INTO BATTLE!

By the same author

RUN OUT THE GUNS
GIVE FIRE!

INTO BATTLE!

A Commander Lord
Charles Oakshott novel

ROBERT CHALLONER

C

CENTURY
LONDON MELBOURNE AUCKLAND JOHANNESBURG

First published in Great Britain in 1987 by
Century Hutchinson Ltd
Brookmount House, 62–65 Chandos Place
London WC2N 4NW

Century Hutchinson South Africa (Pty) Ltd
PO Box 337, Bergvlei, 2012 South Africa

Century Hutchinson Australia Pty Ltd
PO Box 496, 16–22 Church Street, Hawthorn
Victoria 3122, Australia

Century Hutchinson New Zealand Limited
PO Box 40–086, Glenfield, Auckland 10
New Zealand

ISBN 0 7126 1466 4

Printed in Great Britain by
WBC Print Ltd, Bristol

And all I ask is a merry yarn from a laughing
  fellow-rover,
And quiet sleep and a sweet dream when the long
  trick's over.

John Masefield – 'Sea-Fever'

PROLOGUE

Nelson's victory at the Nile wrecked Bonaparte's ambition to use Egypt as his first stepping stone in striding to India like a colossus. Ever a man to cut his losses, the thirty-year-old Corsican adventurer coolly turned his massive driving force elsewhere: callously abandoning his army of thirty-four thousand to death or capture, he slipped back to France in the fastest frigate afloat, and within a month had himself made First Consul and virtual dictator.

The victor of Abu Quir bay was created Baron Nelson of the Nile and Burnham Thorpe (his friends Sir William and Lady Hamilton were furious that he was not raised to a viscountcy, but that honour was to follow).

For his brilliant, but largely unrecorded part in the events leading up to and including the triumph of 1 August 1798,* Charles Oakshott was promoted Captain and given command of the 30-gun *Meteor*, and afterwards *Javelin*, 32 guns – both of which frigates saw useful, if unspectacular, maid-of-all-work service in the Channel approaches, Biscay and the western Mediterranean.

*See *Give Fire!* by Robert Challoner (Century 1986)

Part One

THE SWORD OF DAMOCLES

ONE

'*Gunfire fine on the starboard bow, sir* – close!'

The hail came from the lookout. Night was falling. A boisterous wind from the south-west, promising storm, was pushing *Javelin* along at a good pace. The frigate was a day out of Gibraltar, with Cape Trafalgar abeam, the sea grey and wintry, and every man on deck with two sets of small-clothes crammed under every item of top gear he possessed.

'Very good!' The officer of the watch, too, had heard the crack of a cannon through the gathering storm but it paid to reward attentiveness to duty with a nod and a wink. 'Pass the word to the captain,' he said to the midshipman at his side. 'And beat to quarters.'

Oakshott had flung on his boat cloak and was on deck while the kettle drums were still clattering through the long vessel and men were swarming like lice to their battle stations below and aloft. He took up his place on the quarter-deck and trained his glass in the direction in which everyone was looking and pointing.

'There it goes again, sir,' said someone. 'A sixteen-pounder, no more.'

The homely squeal and rumble of the guns being run out was almost immediately followed by a voice from the companionway, as the elongated features of Lieutenant Thomas A. Brewster appeared over the coaming.

'All guns ready, sir,' intoned the former colonial.

'Very good, Number One,' responded Oakshott.

'Sail ahead and to starboard!' From the bows.

'Steady as you go, helmsman,' said Oakshott. 'And nothing to starboard.'

'Aye, aye, sir.'

Almost immediately following came the cry: 'Another sail – close alongside the first!'

For the men on *Javelin*'s quarter-deck, the sight of it began for all the world like a mountain of washing hung to dry up the face of a Neapolitan tenement building, then quickly hardening into the shape of a well-garnished bowsprit and foremast, next a mainmast followed by a mizzen, and then it was a blunt-bowed, unhandy merchantman wallowing in irons on the frigate's starboard bow – with another, smaller vessel made fast alongside.

'The merchantman's flying Danish colours, sir,' declared the midshipman of the watch. 'T'other's an armed cutter – looks like one of ours. Yes – she's flying the White.' The unformed, eager face was turned questioningly to his captain. 'Boarding the Dane to search for contraband, would she be about, sir?'

'Undoubtedly, Mr Cobbold,' responded Oakshott. 'But who is raising objections, I wonder?'

Oakshott was soon answered, for, with a sudden change in circumstances that could only be likened to coming upon an open glade in the heart of an almost impenetrable wood, the massed clouds suddenly parted and the very last of the wintry daylight revealed the immediate vicinity to the men on *Javelin*'s deck. The Britishers were awakened to the fact that, apart from themselves, the merchantman, and the cutter flying the White Ensign of the Royal Navy, there were four other vessels in close proximity, to wit: two more merchant ships of similar size to the first, another British armed cutter – and a smallish sloop of around 20 guns. Even as Oakshott aimed his glass towards the latter, a blossoming of white gunsmoke from its waist marked the firing of another round – and he saw a cloud of pulverized wood and cordage rise and fall upon the impact of a round shot against the guard rails of the cutter's poop.

Oakshott lowered his glass and slammed it shut. 'Steady as you go, helmsman,' he grated in a dangerously inflected voice. 'Mr Cobbold, will you pass the word to the first lieutenant that I should like that sloop's mizzen topgallant over the side, if he would oblige.'

It is not recorded with what wry amusement Lieutenant Thomas A. Brewster of the Commonwealth of Massachusetts received his captain's ironic order, but the American swiftly acknowledged the same by giving fire with the two for'ard 24-pounders, and bets were made at very short odds – payable in sippers of issue grog – as most of the ship's company watched the two polished spheres of iron rise to their apogee at the very highest part of the sloop's after mast; and a cheer rang out as the upper third section of the mast, hammered out of its seating as if by a giant's fist, fell in a cat's cradle of tangled cordage and sail.

Moments later, the Danish ensign was lowered at the taffrail; nor was this a cowardly act of easy submission, for the harsh geometry of length and breadth plus sail-area, coupled with the strict arithmetic of fire-power and weight of shot, dictated that for the sloop to attempt battle against the frigate would have been like setting a whippet against a greyhound in a foot race, or a terrier against a bull mastiff in a close fight.

'Call away a boarding party,' said Oakshott, and, upon reflection: 'No, I'll go over there myself and see what this is all about.'

It did not call for the exercise of any considerable thought process for Oakshott to realize that this encounter off the Straits of Gibraltar was connected with the trouble that had been brewing between Great Britain and the Baltic states following upon the former's war with France, when the strategic requirements of the belligerents did not always match up with the interests of peaceful trade in the area. Indeed, so fraught with the clash of national interests had seagoing commerce become that the Baltic states had banded together and had adopted a principle of 'Armed Neutrality', which meant in effect that ships of neutral powers should be allowed to trade where they pleased, when they pleased, under the protection of their flags and – if necessary – the guns of their warships.

Though on the face of it a fair principle, it did not operate even-handedly between the two belligerents: Great Britain, an island maritime nation that waged war as much by blockade and embargo as by pitched battle, was put more at a disadvantage by Armed Neutrality than was continental France.

Together with his American first lieutenant and others, Oakshott had been fortunate enough to retain his servant Bantock throughout his commissioning of *Meteor* and *Javelin*. A survivor of the old *Daisy*, the formidable Bantock, anticipating his captain's requirements, had laid out Oakshott's dress uniform coat, clean shirt, nankeen breeches, silk stockings and waistcoat, in readiness to overawe the Danes.

'Tell my secretary to lay aft,' ordered Oakshott, kicking off his heavy seaboots and dropping the coarse sailcloth pantaloons that he affected at sea in the winter.

'Aye, aye, sir.' Bantock scooped up boots and nether garment and doubled away to do his master's bidding.

Oakshott was fastening the black stock about his throat when the captain's secretary of HMS *Javelin* entered after a discreet knock. The entry, as ever, was done with a distinctive style. Pepe Lopez, a Spanish Moor born in Cadiz, educated by the imams of the Saracenic university and also by the Jesuits, was a man of parts and of most liberal attainments. Captured and enslaved by Corsair pirates, his family murdered or dispersed, he had risen above these vicissitudes and retained a remarkable good humour. He was also devoted to Charles Oakshott. It was a devotion founded upon experience of the latter's qualities in good times and bad.

'Sir, you summoned me.' The secretary stood by the door, clad in the habiliments of clerical grey that he affected, a twinkle of attentiveness in his berry-black, clever eyes.

'Pepe, you'll accompany me over to the Danish sloop,' replied Oakshott. 'Do you speak the lingo?'

'I do not, sir,' responded the other. 'However, I think you will find that most Balts are conversant with English. Or German. And I am fluent in the latter, as the Captain is aware.'

Oakshott nodded, adjusting his dress sword to his hip. 'Good,' he said. 'In any event, I want you with me to be witness to any possible awkwardness. This Armed Neutrality has raised many a brouhaha recently, and I don't want to be involved in an Admiralty court, nor hauled over the coals by the unwieldy workings of maritime law.'

The clever eyes flashed intelligence. 'You refer to the well-placed cannon shot to the Danishman's topmast, sir,' said Lopez. 'But, surely, that was quite in order, since the other party had already fired upon the White Ensign.'

'That's as may be, Pepe,' responded Oakshott, picking up his Nile medal on its watered silk ribbon, regarding it thoughtfully for a moment and then looping it round his neck. 'But one is sailing in murky waters with this Armed Neutrality – and there are lawyers in plenty hanging around the Admiralty court in the happy anticipation of picking up a few guineas for acting against the interests of their own country by pleading the case of some damned neutral who has had a shot fired across his bow to the discomfiture of the ship's cat.'

He picked up his boat cloak and hat. 'Let's go, Pepe,' he said.

Smiling, Pepe Lopez followed his captain out of the stern cabin and on to the waiting boat.

He's not liking this, said the secretary to himself. Rather than confront that Danish skipper, our Charlie would sail straight at a French battle fleet with all guns blazing.

The crew of the *Javelin*'s gig tossed oars at the midshipman's command beneath the lowering side of the Danish sloop. Watchful for the slightest sign that his captain might find anything amiss with his performance as coxswain, the boy officer eyed Oakshott with some trepidation.

'Lie off and pick us up in due course,' said Oakshott, and he preceded Pepe Lopez up the accommodation ladder.

The deck officer, who did not have him piped aboard, spoke no English, but intimated by gestures that Oakshott might care to follow him aft. This the *Javelin*'s captain did, remarking to himself how the mizzen topgallant still hung in its tangle of cordage, further subtracting from the sailing qualities of the sloop by obstructing the functions of the mizzen lateen; nor was there any sign of attempts being made to cut the spar free. Perhaps, thought Oakshott, they intended to keep it there as some kind of evidence against him.

That the sloop's captain awaited his attendance below instead of being on deck to greet him quite accorded with Oakshott's own method of dealing with 'awkward visitors'; nor was he put out of countenance one whit by the pantomime – obviously precontrived – of his guide tapping on the door of the stern cabin and awaiting the pointedly protracted pause before a gruff voice from beyond bade them enter.

The appearance of the sloop's after cabin was so poignantly reminiscent of his own, late quarters aboard his first command, HM sloop-of-war *Daisy*, as to be almost like coming home: of similar dimensions, its unaccommodating shape dictated the number and placements of the very few items of furniture. Immediately facing the door was an almost identical desk-cum-dining table from behind which the Danish captain was rising to his feet in sullen greeting; while to his left, on the starboard quarter, was the familiar shape of a let-down bunk that also occasionally served as a daytime sofa: Oakshott registered from the corner of his eye that it was presently occupied by a figure in black.

The uniformed man behind the desk was tall and flaxen-haired like a Viking, five years or so younger than Oakshott and – immediately discernible to the latter – extremely angry, as he introduced himself in the German language, which Pepe Lopez immediately translated:

'Lieutenant Lehmann, captain of the sloop-of-war *Hedeby*, sir. And he says that . . .'

'I can imagine what he says,' responded Oakshott. 'Tell him, however, that I'm sorry to have fired upon him, but he will appreciate that I had no alternative in the circumstances. He was shooting at one of His Britannic Majesty's ships . . .'

He was interrupted by a tirade from the Dane, which was presently relayed to him by his secretary:

'The captain says that the ship was attempting to board one of the merchantmen sailing under the flag of a neutral state, and in convoy under his protection, sir.'

'Tell him that the ship in question was performing its duty as an armed vessel of a declared belligerent nation,' responded Oakshott. 'And was determining if the said merchantman was carrying goods that might be of use or comfort to the king's enemies, either directly or indirectly.'

This was conveyed to Lehmann, and the answer came back:

'The captain says that, under the principles of Armed Neutrality, Denmark does not accept a belligerent's right to make a forcible boarding of . . .'

It was here that Pepe Lopez was cut short by a drawling voice coming from Oakshott's left:

'The principles cannot be enforced today. Today, it is the larger cannon that rules!'

They all turned to face the speaker – the figure that lounged among cushions on the let-down cot; one elegant leg crossed over the other, a manicured hand resting negligently on the backboard, suavely barbered head set on one side; archly eyeing first one and then the other of the two ship's captains through a quizzing glass.

'Lieutenant Lehmann has neglected to introduce me,' he said. 'In the circumstances, a pardonable error. Count Axel Bernstorff – at your service.'

'Oakshott,' responded the other, acknowledging the other man with a stiff bow, to which the recipient responded in a like manner. They eyed each other warily for a few moments, and Oakshott was uncannily aware of being in the presence of a considerable intellectual force, an almost overwhelming personality.

Aged – Oakshott reckoned him at about thirty-five. Middling tall, as near as could be judged from his sitting posture. Dark for a Scandinavian, but with the most iridescent blue eye he had ever seen – and it was literally *one* eye; the other was covered with a black eye-patch. Black, also, was his coat of figured silk, the breeches and stockings, the waistcoat. Only frilled white lawn at slender wrists and below the black silk stock that banded the elegant throat relieved the funereal effect – that, and diamond buckles that winked with every movement of Count Bernstorff's neatly shod feet, and the replica of an order of knighthood – fashioned of silver and gold lace and diamonds – which embellished the left breast of his coat.

'I repeat,' said the aristocrat, 'it is the size of the guns which carries the day. I would suggest, Captain Oakshott, that you yourself search the convoy forthwith, and satisfy yourself that they carry no contraband.'

'That, unfortunately is now out of the question, sir,' replied Oakshott. 'Night has fallen and a storm is blowing up. Such a move would have to wait for both daylight and a calmer sea.'

'Then what alternative proposal do you have in mind?' It was almost a taunt, and delivered with another look through the glass.

'I should be prepared to accept Lieutenant Lehmann's parole,' said Oakshott. 'If he pledges to put into Gibraltar tomorrow and submit himself to a search, that will adequately meet the needs of my Admiralty's instructions.'

Another look through the quizzing glass. 'And is the solemn word of a Danish officer sufficient to meet your needs, Lord Charles?'

Oakshott, surprised that a foreigner, moreover a complete stranger, should address him by his courtesy title, could only nod agreement.

Framed by the carefully coiffed raven's wing of hair, the smooth, pale-complexioned face permitted the ghost of a smile to ruffle its obviously accustomed gravity.

'That being settled,' said Count Axel Bernstorff, 'let us take wine together, gentlemen.'

They made a curious foursome, taking wine, ill-assorted as they were.

Lehmann, taciturn and sullen, drank deeply and quickly, constantly replenishing his glass and scowling over its rim at the man who had taken off his mizzen topgallant, nor did he ask Pepe Lopez to translate any of the conversation in English that was taking place between Bernstorff and Oakshott. For his part, Pepe tried a few pleasantries in German, but the one-sided connection swiftly languished from lack of support.

The discourse between the other two, on the contrary, was brisk and lively. Bernstorff knew England well, mixed in

London Society, and appeared familiar with the structure of British nobility: he certainly knew Oakshott's antecedents, and the fact that only a rather sickly five-year-old nephew stood between him and the Marquisate of Uffingham and Bow, Sennett Palace and all. He seemed to think that this was an enviable state of affairs; Oakshott did not feel it necessary to disabuse him on this account.

Clearly a man to be reckoned with. But what was he doing in a sloop-of-war on the way to the Med? He decided to ask . . .

In answer to Oakshott's carefully phrased inquiry, Bernstorff tapped his chest and allowed his austere features to soften in a tired smile that carried overtones of mild self-indulgence – which reminded the Englishman that even the most impressive of personalities have their minor defects of character.

'I am travelling to the Mediterranean for my health, sir,' he replied. 'The chest – I suffered from a slight consumption of the lungs when young, and the affliction still pursues me. Northern Europe is an anathema to me in the winter, but not till now have I been able to rid myself of my obligations and flee to whatever warmth I am able to find in the North African littoral. As to my means of transport – I am here by grace and favour of my cousin, the Secretary to the Danish Board of Admiralty.'

A hypochondriac, thought Oakshott, and softened towards the otherwise daunting character. And the secretary cousin accounts for him dictating the movements of Danish ships, he added.

Aloud, he said: 'Count, I think that we must now make our departure, for I am due with all speed to Portsmouth.'

They shook hands. A reiteration of his regret for being obliged to fire upon the *Hedeby* won for him yet another scowl and a growl from her captain.

A hail brought the *Javelin*'s jollyboat alongside. Oakshott descended into the boat behind Pepe Lopez. As the oarsmen gave stroke and they made way across the grey waters, Oakshott looked back to see the figure in black watching them from the quarter-deck of the sloop. Even at that distance, the man's powerful presence struck him most forcibly.

There was a ship's boat lying off *Javelin*, and the reason for it greeted Oakshott when he climbed aboard his command, to find a scowling individual in common sailor's slops who introduced himself as Lieutenant Jakeman, commanding officer of *Mole*, the armed cutter which *Hedeby* had fired upon. By the fellow's attitude, it was clear that he was far from pleased.

'I see that you've been aboard the Danish sloop,' he growled, omitting the courtesy of a 'sir'. 'So what's to be done now?'

'The matter is closed,' said Oakshott, who knew a tricky customer when he saw one. 'Honours are even. You suffered a hit. I hit them. Tit for tat. Now we all go on our ways and you continue with your patrol.'

The other's close-set eyes narrowed beneath beetling brows. A thoroughly unpleasant character, thought Oakshott. Came up to a King's Commission via the lower deck, one wouldn't wonder – and immediately felt unworthy for the thought.

'What about their contraband, then?' demanded Jakeman.

'I put their captain on parole to enter Gibraltar tomorrow and be searched,' he replied.

'And I suppose you think he'll honour his promise,' sneered the other.

'Of course.'

'Well, you've got more faith in the honour of so-called gentlemen than I have,' was the response. 'I bid you good night – *sir*.'

Without more ado, the cutter's captain gave Oakshott a sketchy approximation to a salute and went over the side to his waiting boat.

'Oh, dear me,' murmured Oakshott to himself. 'There goes a fellow who does not repose much trust in your judgement, Charlie.'

By now it was pitch-black night. The south-westerly was showing every promise of turning into a full gale. The group of ships re-formed into their various parts, each going their separate ways: the Danes to the east and the distant pillars of Hercules, there to fulfil the terms of the parole that the mysterious Count Axel Bernstorff had endorsed, the small Royal Navy flotilla resuming its patrol of the western approaches to the Straits, little damage of note having been caused by the *Hedeby*'s single hit on the cutter; Oakshott gave orders to shape course through Biscay on the highly favourable wind.

He remained up on deck till the last of the Danish convoy dipped out of sight; Pepe Lopez stood by him.

'An odd character, that Bernstorff,' mused Oakshott.

'I wonder if he's trustworthy, sir,' said Lopez.

Oakshott glanced sharply at his secretary. 'Why do you say that?' he demanded.

The other looked down at his fingernails. 'Only that – or so it seemed to me – one never actually *heard* him pass on the order to Lieutenant Lehmann to put into Gibraltar, sir. And Lehmann certainly never understood a word of your conversation.'

'And what do you deduce from that?'

'Well, sir,' said Lopez, 'if Lehmann had given his parole to put into Gibraltar, as arranged, he might – upon his word as an officer – feel obliged in honour to keep his word.'

'But Bernstorff might not – is that what you imply?'

Pepe Lopez shrugged his narrow shoulders. 'As you said, sir, he strikes one as an odd sort of character.'

Oakshott regarded his companion for a few moments before responding, taking in the canny, complex characteristics that birth, upbringing and frightful experience had marked upon the other's countenance: in his untrusting, berry-black eyes, in the cynical curve of his mouth.

'I think you may be over-subtle in this regard, Pepe,' he said. 'When all's been said and done, there are times when a gentleman must be taken at his word, be he officer or no.' He smiled, patted the other on the shoulder and turned to face the wind. 'We'll be in for a real blow tonight,' he declared. 'But it will push us on to Pompey in fine style.'

Pepe Lopez watched his captain stride to the break of the quarter-deck, where, steadying his tall form against the mainmast chains from the kick of the sea, he looked out towards the receding lights of the other vessels.

'Over-subtle I may be, Charlie,' said the Spanish Moor, only half aloud, 'but it takes *two* gentlemen to make good an unwritten bond.

'And I saw in that Danish hidalgo the look of a Corsair pirate, and the craft of an oily auctioneer in the slave market of Algiers.'

TWO

HMS *Javelin* made the Solent in spanking time, with one man lost overboard and a broken jib boom to tell of her furious run before the sou'westerlies. Upon arrival in Portsmouth, she secured alongside the Hard, and Oakshott went to collect his letters and report to the office of the admiral commanding. There he was informed that *Javelin* was to shift at once to Buckler's Hard to undergo a swift refit for further service unspecified.

Mindful of the disturbing contents of some of the letters he had found awaiting his return, Oakshott decided to leave command of the short journey to Buckler's in the capable hands of First Lieutenant Brewster – a pledge of trust and an opportunity which the ambitious American officer was pleased to seize in both hands.

Oakshott waited long enough to watch his ship warping out into the ebb for her brief voyage down the Solent, then took coach for London and an onward journey to the home of his ancestors – which he had not seen for over two long years.

Upon reaching the massive wrought-iron gates of Sennett – both of them sagging drunkenly open on broken hinges – Oakshott paid off the carriage that he had taken from the posting inn, ordering the coachman to drop his traps at the main door of the palace. He then set off to walk the last quarter of a mile home and see for himself what further depredations had befallen the estate during his absence.

To start with, both gatehouses – thanks to lack of funds for repairing their roofs – were now half in ruin, windowless, doorless and abandoned. His sister-in-law had written him that the two old married couples – former servants and estate workers who had enjoyed free board and lodgings and a pittance for keeping symbolic watch and ward over the entrance gates – had had to be dismissed, presumably to beggary.

The walk up the long, curving drive towards the bank of great elms that partly hid the worst of the mansion's derelictions from the visitor provided further evidence of ill fortune. Due no doubt to lack of paid labour, no hay had been cut the previous year. A fine stand of mature willows down by the stew pond had been felled and sold to pay for the young marquess to be taken to Bath for the waters – as Oakshott had been informed. On the other hand, pheasants abounded, there being no man in residence to shoot them; the homecomer made a firm resolve to put that matter to rights.

One last bend in the drive brought into sight the ill-favoured Baroque pile that a grateful monarch and country had provided for Alexander Oakshott, First Marquess of Uffingham and Bow in recognition of his services to Charles I at the battle of Marston Moor and those of his ravishing wife Eulalia to Charles II elsewhere. It was set in a disastrous site in swampy ground below the Lambourn downs, and it seemed to Charles Oakshott's keenly nautical eye that the vast building and its central dome were declining ever more to starboard and that the main roof ridge had taken on a decided sag amidships.

His traps – having been set down on the top of the great flight of marble steps leading to the carved proscenium of the great front door and tympanum garnished with gesticulating figures – had apprised his sister-in-law of his imminent arrival.

'Charlie – how wonderful to see you!'

She flew into his arms and he embraced her, a transaction which made plain to him that Harriet had put on a little weight whilst he had been away – and to some advantage.

'Why did you not write me you had arrived back in England?' she cried, disengaging her lips from his. 'The first I knew was the fellow hammering on the door with news of your baggage.'

'We put in only on Tuesday,' explained Oakshott, 'and I took post right away.' He searched her face. 'And I read your letters awaiting me in Pompey,' he added.

She avoided his eye. In such a manner had she shown her natural modesty on the day that he had put it to her – daughter of an impoverished widow to an archdeacon, reduced to singing popular ballads in the admittedly respectable Mogg's Diversions in the Strand – that she might do worse for herself than marry his brother and make herself Marchioness of Uffingham and Bow. Harriet had shown great circumspection in not rushing into this superficially attractive offer – the more particularly when she had set eyes on the intended groom, who had been reduced by drink and general debauchery to the state of a fat, puking loon; but she had finally accepted, and to give the lass her due had made the best of a bad bargain. Released by time's effluxion from the presence of her husband, who now lay in a marble sarcophagus, together with his ancestors in the family chapel, she was all alone with her five-year-old son, the seventh marquess.

The arrival on the scene of Struthers, the incredibly ancient butler and general factotum of Sennett, along with two kitchen lads to pick up Oakshott's luggage, saved Harriet from making any further comment there and then; instead, she led her brother-in-law upstairs to her sitting room, the bow window of which looked out across the jungle of what had been a formal garden after the Versailles manner. In this room, furnished with the best of what remained in the palace, together with such minor masterpieces of Dutch and English painting as had not been sold, did the dowager marchioness spend most of her days at her books and her embroidery. In one corner of the room stood a spinet, testimony to Harriet's continuing talent for singing to her own accompaniment.

She motioned her brother-in-law to be seated, and brought a decanter of brandy from a corner cupboard, pouring them both a bumper measure.

They pledged each other, raising their glasses in silence, their eyes meeting.

'I've seen you only once, and that briefly, since your return from the Nile,' she said, her eyes slipping away from his glance. 'Your letters are very spare. Tell me what you've been about.'

'Routine patrols and convoy duty,' said Oakshott, shrugging. 'Little action. No glory. Nor any prize money – more's the pity.' He observed that the figured silk wall-covering over the bow window was streaked with rust mould and peeling away. And he readdressed himself to his drink.

'And you have not asked me about little Charlie,' she said.

'I was about to,' he countered. 'How is the lad?'

'The same – and growing more like you every day, Charlie,' she said softly. 'The nursemaid will be bringing him up as soon as he's had his supper, so you'll see for yourself.'

'That will be very nice,' he said.

Silence.

'Touching upon my letters,' said Harriet.

'Ah, yes.'

'What are your views, Charlie, as regards my proposal?'

'To marry the gentleman you mentioned?'

'Yes.'

Observing a fleck of lint on the skirt of his uniform coat, Oakshott carefully removed it with finger and thumb and thoughtfully watched the thing flutter to the floor.

'You hold this gentleman – Mr – er? . . .'

'Jarvis – Mr Henry Jarvis. Of Marlborough.'

'Do you hold Mr Jarvis in great affection?'

'I esteem him quite highly.'

'Esteem – ah, that's important.'

Harriet got up and walked to the window. The view out on to the ruined formal garden not providing her with the stimulus she sought, she presently went over to the spinet and sat down there, regarding the silent keys.

'There's naught else for it, Charlie,' she said. 'Penniless widows with offspring are not at a premium nowadays. Not even penniless marchionesses. Any man with a reasonably sized purse has only to look at Sennett and he runs like a hare.'

'But Mr Jarvis has a capacious purse, or so you indicated.'

'He is esteemed the richest man in the county.'

'Where are his estates, Harriet?'

'He has no estates. A town house in Marlborough. And a country house with a few acres – that's all. He positively yearns to restore Sennett to its former glory.'

'Does he, now?' mused Oakshott, and forbore to give his opinion that the former glory of Sennett was of a very illusory sort; scarcely had the mansion been built – upon a marsh – than the cellars, at least, were rendered unusable.

'I need hardly add, Charlie,' said his sister-in-law, 'that if such a thing came to pass, it would take an intolerable burden from my mind. And you have only to consider the difference it would make to little Charlie's prospects.'

Oakshott nodded agreement, being fully in sympathy with her.

'And what is the source of Mr Jarvis's wealth?' he asked.

'He is a self-made man – through trade.'

'Trade – *ah!*'

He saw her hackles rise, and also perceived that she had been mistaken in his reaction to her news. Indeed, she positively flared up at him.

'I, who was not born into the ermine,' she cried, 'but only the child of a humble churchman, do not have your aristocratic contempt for those who have earned their crust by honest enterprise!'

Oakshott smiled. 'You have me in error, Harriet,' he said. 'As to my aristocratic birth, I have to remind you that my ancestor, the first marquess, was a soldier of fortune. His lady wife, the alluring Eulalia, was – not to put too fine a point on it – a strumpet, though of the very highest and most expensive sort.

'No, Harriet, if I exclaim in surprise, it is only out of admiration for someone who could make himself the richest man in the county through trade. *What* trade, might I ask?'

'Leather tanning.' Her chin was up: she was still on the defensive.

'Leather tanning.' He nodded. 'I must remember that. A good and prosperous occupation if or when I am ever disabled and have to quit the navy.'

Harriet's expression softened at once, and her hand stole out to take hold of his. 'Charlie, it is my earnest hope and prayer that such a thing will never happen to you,' she said. 'Indeed, it is for you, as much as for little Charlie and myself, that I yearn to put Sennett and the estate to rights and remove for ever its burden from the shoulders of the Oakshotts.'

'That's a very noble aspiration, Harriet,' he said, with a tenderness he felt very strongly.

Again, she strayed towards the window, and remained there with her back to him.

'Mr Jarvis is all that a woman could wish in a husband,' she said. 'He is kind and gentle. Not well educated, but of great sensibility. We get on well together – notwithstanding the disparity in our ages . . .'

'How old is he, Harriet?' asked Oakshott, feeling that they were coming to the nub of the dialogue.

'He is twenty-two years my senior.'

'Ah . . .'

Oakshott was spared any further comment by a tap upon the door, which then opened to admit a small boy in a sailor suit. Dark-haired and pale, he was holding the hand of a young nursemaid.

'Come to say good night, your ladyship,' said the girl. 'We've 'ad our supper, an' we ate it up like a good boy.'

'Come to me, Charlie,' said his mother. 'Come, and say hello to your uncle.'

The boy advanced with a quite remarkable gravity, kissed his mother and, with scarcely more than a nod and a prod from her by way of prompting, turned to the tall figure in the gold-laced coat and held out a hand.

'Good evening, Uncle,' he said. 'I trust . . .'

'That you had . . .' from Harriet.

'That you had a pleasant journey to Sennett.'

'I did, Charlie, I did, and thank you,' responded the other, taking the small hand in his and finding it piteously frail, small-boned and delicate as the body of a bird.

And the eyes that gazed up at him: one brown, one blue – a legacy of the illustrious beauty Eulalia, carried on the male line with a few interruptions. It was like looking into his own shaving mirror. Oakshott felt a lump coming to his throat, and his own parti-coloured eyes prickled treacherously.

'Is he not very like you, Charlie?' asked the boy's mother. 'A true Oakshott.'

There was no denying it. In such a sailor suit was he himself not brought, each eve, to this very room, to bid his mother good night? Nor was he then, surely, any more robust than little Charlie here? The dank miasmas of Sennett made it no place to rear the young.

Never entirely at ease with children, with whom he had had little congress, Oakshott eyed the young marquess with his head on one side and essayed a little pleasantry.

'And now tell me, Charlie,' he said, 'do you have any fancy to be a sailor when you grow up?'

'No, I don't, sir,' was the immediate response. 'When I grow up, I'm going to be a jockey.'

'Oh, are you?' commented Oakshott, a bit out of countenance.

'He was taken to the horse races at Epsom in the summer,' explained Harriet, fondly tousling her son's dark mane of hair. 'Before then, he wanted to drive the mail coach to London.'

'A jockey – that's what I'm going to be,' reiterated the boy.*

'Well, what do you think, Charlie?' asked Harriet.

It was ten o'clock. Old Struthers had just cleared away supper.

Oakshott was pacing up and down the room: fifteen paces one way and back again – turn – and repeat. This brought him shy of the end wall by at least ten feet, but the length of Harriet's sitting room exceeded the length of *Javelin*'s quarter-deck by just that much. Ingrained habits die hard.

'Do you approve?' she added. 'You, after all, in little Charlie's minority, are head of the family.'

'I think,' said Oakshott, ceasing his perambulations, 'that the decision must be yours, Harriet. I have nothing to offer to weigh in the scales of your judgement, being engaged upon a profession of war which might turn me off at any time. And penniless in the bargain.'

'Is there no more you can add to that, Charlie?' she asked.

Oakshott saw the beginnings of a squall that might presage a storm and bring him to destruction on the rocks. After the manner of his profession, he turned and made for deeper waters.

'There might be, at that, Harriet,' he responded. 'But I

*This anecdote appears in the autobiography of Rear Admiral Charles Oakshott, seventh Marquess of Uffingham and Bow, VC, KCB, RN (1794–1885) in the chapter relating to his beloved 'Uncle Charlie'.

should have to give it some thought. Yes, I should have to sleep on it, at least.'

She eyed him steadily. 'As you please,' she said. 'And would it not clarify your thoughts, perhaps, if we first brought into the open certain – factors – and one in particular that we have scarcely touched upon these last two years since my husband, your brother Jack, died.'

Under the darkening sky, with the storm almost upon him, Oakshott metaphorically reefed all sail and streamed a sea anchor to ride out the tempest.

'Not tonight, Harriet,' he said. 'It has been a long day for me. If you don't mind, I should like to turn in, the better to bring my thoughts to a point tomorrow.'

She nodded. But grudgingly. 'You have your old room prepared,' she said. 'And the roof has been made good with the money left over from the sale of the willows.'

He took up a candelabrum from the table.

'Good night, then, Harriet,' he said.

She turned to face him squarely. Every inch the archdeacon's daughter: proud, austere, withdrawn. But all woman underneath.

'Sleep well, Charlie,' she said.

His room in the south wing, reached by way of one of the curving corridors that flanked the main block of the palace, smelt sweeter than when he was last there. The plaster ceiling showed signs of having been patched, though the money had not run to remoulding the fine cornice work. The bed was made, the sheets clean, and a warming pan laid within. Oakshott undressed, put on his nightshirt, shirked his prayers, poured himself a measure of brandy from the flask in his valise and climbed in between the sheets.

Five years and more . . .

Was it so long ago, that winter when, returning from the bloody rout of Toulon, his best friend killed, he had been alone in London and, like many a lonely sailor and soldier before him, had yearned for company – any company.

Naturally, his footsteps had taken him to Mogg's Diversions, and there was Harriet – for she had run away from brother Jack and from Sennett.

It had been a tearful meeting, for Harriet had known – perhaps loved – his dead comrade Ned. Thrown together by a common bond of grief and loneliness, with a blizzard scouring the streets outside, their thoughts had turned to the comfort of mutual warmth.

'I've lodgings in a basement in Pimlico, Charlie . . . it isn't far . . .'

Nine months to that night, Harriet gave birth to the heir of Uffingham and Bow, and brother Jack had rejoiced. His wife returned, a strapping son delivered to him – though by what means his drink-befuddled mind could not encompass – he had accepted little Charlie without question as his own.

With a sigh Oakshott reached out and took from his bedside table the *Book of Common Prayer* that he carried with him always. Presented to him by his mother when he had first gone to sea as a midshipman of fourteen, it had been his constant companion in good times and bad; from it he had read innumerable Orders for the Burial of the Dead at Sea; on at least three occasions, the Form of Solemnization of Matrimony. Such are the prerogatives of a ship's captain of the Royal Navy.

He turned – slowly and cautiously, the way a cat will approach a bowl of cream – to the last page, which was headed:

A TABLE OF KINDRED AND AFFINITY
Wherein Whosoever are Related are Forbidden in Scripture and our Laws to Marry Together . . .

Not for the first time, he sought out the solution that he

knew he would never find. All thirty conditions as applied to a man. And similarly for a woman.

A Man may not marry his . . .
25. Brother's Daughter,
26. Sister's daughter,
27. Brother's Son's wife.

This was all that applied to one's brother or sister; nothing about being forbidden, either by canon or civil law, from marrying one's brother's wife.

And Harriet knew that as well as he.

The raucous cry of a cock pheasant down in the south copse greeted Oakshott's wakefulness and prompted him to get out of bed, wash himself in a basin of cold water, slip into warm apparel of civilian fustian and make his way down to the gun room – a small apartment set off at the end of the banner-hung great hall.

Brother Jack had never been one for active sports save those of the boudoir, and their father's and grandfather's collection of fine sporting guns had not been kept in the prime condition which they deserved. Nevertheless, Oakshott was able to satisfy himself that one of the brace of long Kentucky smooth-bores which a military cousin had brought back from the Revolutionary War and presented to the fifth marquess was in fair order, with a newish flint, a clean and slightly oiled barrel free of rust. And the very feel and balance of the excellent weapon were an inspiration.

It was chill out in the park. The grass was white with hoar frost and the air tasted like vanilla water ice. Skirting the main block and the stable, Oakshott moved towards the south copse in a slanting course which might fool any pheasant into thinking that he was merely a passing acquaintance.

Fifty yards from the edge of the copse, a cock pheasant –

possibly his clarion – rose screeching from under his very feet. A dog would have brought it up at a better distance. Oakshott, coming up on aim, hesitated to fire immediately for fear of spoiling the bird. Pulled the trigger. It was a misfire. By the time he had cocked again, the pheasant was gliding down to triumphant safety in the next field.

And then he saw – *her* . . .

She came round the side of the copse, mounted on a chestnut. She came like Primavera, riding down the winter landscape. Or Diana the huntress, chaste and fair. Fair of complexion, blonde as a Valkyrie, tall in the saddle, straight as a ramrod.

'Charles!' she called out. 'They told me in the village that you were back. How very nice to see you, my dear.'

He doffed his hat and reached up to take her proffered hand.

'Irene – how wonderful you look.'

This was possibly the only woman in Oakshott's life who had ever shaken him half out of his firm resolve never to marry and in one stroke both spoil another person's life and his own unswerving allegiance to the seafaring vocation. Irene Chancellor, widow of one of his boyhood friends, had always possessed the power to move him in a way that he with his deeply analytical mind found totally inexplicable. No coquette, straight as a die, incapable of dissembling, she nevertheless remained to him a complete enigma of allurement.

'I trust, Charles, that you will find time to call upon me before you go back to sea again.'

'Most assuredly, Irene,' he said. 'When will it be convenient?'

Her unbelievably lustrous green eyes swept over him. She touched a damask cheek with a gloved fingertip and pursed her lips in thought.

'You could come to dinner tonight,' she said. 'But that is quite a long time hence.'

He thought he discerned the turn of her humour. 'Madame, it is an eternity,' he said.

'On the other hand, afternoon tea is not to your taste.'

'I have never been a one for tea.'

She frowned and shook her head. 'And I already have an engagement for luncheon at the rectory. But that is a good four hours from now.'

'And the rector and his lady must not be kept waiting.'

'Sir, we might just have time to take breakfast together – if we hurry.'

Smiling, Oakshott propped his gun up against a tree and placed his hat over the muzzle to protect the bore from any dampness.

'Does that fine-looking chestnut carry two, Irene?' he asked.

'He never has – but he could learn,' replied she.

Without more ado, Oakshott vaulted up on to the chestnut's broad back behind Irene Chancellor. As his arm enfolded her slender waist, she turned in the saddle and met his lips with hers.

A brief and passionate exchange – and they were away at a smart gallop, the pair of them.

From her bedchamber Harriet, Dowager Marchioness of Uffingham and Bow, let fall the curtain and turned away from the window – as the chestnut and its two riders vanished round the edge of the copse.

Handsome still, even with her hair undressed, and fine of figure in her lace-trimmed peignoir, she crossed over to an easy chair by the fire and, seating herself, stared down into the glowing coals till she seemed to see there the laughing face of Charles Oakshott, and a slow tear coursed down her smooth cheek.

'It's no use,' she whispered aloud. 'And I was a fool to hope otherwise.'

*

A letter from Lieutenant Tom Brewster determined Oakshott's actions for the next three successive Sundays whilst the Banns of Marriage were read in the private chapel of Sennett Palace between Henry Jarvis, Esquire, a widower of the Parish of St Mary the Virgin, Marlborough, and Harriet, Dowager Marchioness of Uffingham and Bow.

His morning's interlude in the company of Irene Chancellor having – in his phrase – 'brought his mind to a point', Oakshott had put it to his sister-in-law that, taking one thing with another, she might do far worse than accept Mr Jarvis's offer of marriage. Oddly, and much to his surprise – and relief – Harriet had readily agreed.

She, poor lady – who had earlier nursed a hope that, notwithstanding his penniless state and his devotion to the Navy, her brother-in-law might take upon himself the burden of marriage and fatherhood, and join with her in making Sennett prosper by their own efforts – now realized that she might as lief try to cage a skylark and make him happy. And the factor of Irene Chancellor scarcely came into her reckoning.

The letter from his first lieutenant gave Oakshott *carte blanche* to remain and see Harriet safely launched for the second time upon the sea of matrimony . . .

Sir,

I have the honour to report that the ship is now in dry dock at Buckler's Hard and, having been examined, is found to be sound underwater in all respects.

It has been determined, sir, that all masts, spars and standing rigging shall be renewed. The teak deck planking is also in need of renewal, but this will occasion some delay because the supply of seasoned teak is held up. The nearest date I have for completion is five weeks hence . . .

So it was that Harriet was walked up the aisle of Sennett chapel on the arm of her brother-in-law; past the marbled tombs of Oakshotts long gone and under shot-rent banners that spoke of their prowess on many a field of battle. It is likely that the shade of the almost legendary Eulalia – she of the parti-coloured eyes widely distributed among her male descendants – gazed down with approval upon the marchioness who was willing to sacrifice herself (as Eulalia had done, again and again, beyond the call of duty) for the good of Sennett and the succession.

The bride wore figured pink trimmed with white lace and looked five years younger than she was. Her train was carried by the young marquess, her son. Little Charlie was wearing the miniature uniform of a midshipman RN.

Reaching the altar rail, Oakshott handed over his charge to the care of the groom. He had, as a matter of conscience, searched out his prospective brother-in-law by taking him on innumerable tours of the taverns of the county and had found him to be moderate in his cups and showing no proclivity towards the women of the town and serving wenches. Mr Jarvis spoke directly and honestly upon all matters touching on his projected marriage and his intentions towards the estate, which, as he put it, he regarded as being a sacred trust for young Charlie and his heirs.

His function in the ceremony discharged, Oakshott took his seat near the front of the congregation beside Irene Chancellor, who looked ravishing in grey heightened with royal blue.

The Form of Solemnization of Matrimony was carried out by the Rev. Mr Winslow, local rector and chaplain to the marquess. This divine had succeeded the late Rev. Mr Hardcourt-ffinch, a hunting-and-fishing parson who had officiated at Harriet's previous wedding and had on that occasion preached one of the longest sermons on record – largely concerned with the desiderata of present-day hunting. Winslow was of the Fundamentalist persuasion and very devout. His sermon, though scarcely half the length of his predecessor's, was devoted to the evils of Fornication, Adultery, Drunkenness, Blasphemy, Swearing, and not keeping the Sabbath holy; as a disincentive to his listeners, he then described the torments of hellfire in resounding detail.

At the close the bride and groom proceeded down the aisle and out into the wintry sunlight, where they were pelted with petals by the estate tenants and servants, whose habitual sullenness had been subdued by Mr Jarvis's generous gift of a hamper of food and drink to every family and a gold guinea for each and every one.

The worm-eaten Oakshott ceremonial coach having at last been condemned as unfit for use, the bride and groom were conveyed to their front door in a very smart phaeton, and Charles Oakshott breathed a sigh of relief.

'Charles, I am giving a dinner party tomorrow. May I rely upon you to act as my consort and joint host?'

Oakshott dragged himself away from his thoughts to regard the brilliant creature upon his arm.

'Irene, I cannot,' he replied. 'For I've been summoned to the Admiralty by a letter which arrived only this morning.'

She looked disappointed. 'Must you go immediately? Do their lordships summon distinguished ships' captains with such little regard for the civilities – so peremptorily?'

He gave her a rueful smile. 'My dear, I may cut a bit of a dash in this part of Berkshire, but I can assure you that my slender distinction butters no parsnips in the corridors of the Admiralty. And – yes – their lordships are wont to summon anyone they choose, when they choose, and how they choose.' He frowned. 'Only . . .'

'Only – what, Charles?'

'Oh – nothing, my dear.'

Scarcely worth mentioning, he thought to himself. But, still, it was a straw in the wind when a ship's captain was summoned – and, as Irene had put it, peremptorily – by a functionary describing himself as an Admiralty Clerk, Class II.

And the tone of the letter, disregarding its ingredients, was curt to a degree: '. . . *attend, to answer certain questions regarding certain facts which have been presented to their lordships.*' And: '. . . *You will wish to present yourself without delay . . . these matters are pressingly urgent.*'

Yes, things had come to a pretty pass when the captain of a crack frigate could be so addressed by an Admiralty Clerk, Class II – and a civilian to boot.

'Certain questions . . . certain facts.' What questions were those, and what facts?

Oakshott searched his mind for any misdemeanours he might have committed in the recent past – but could think of none. His conscience was clear, he told himself. And with complete conviction.

But Pepe Lopez, that discerning cynic, might have hazarded a guess as to what was awaiting his captain at the Admiralty; for his deeply-ingrained cynicism regarding the conduct of certain of his fellow human beings had already prompted the ex-slave to a possibility that had never occurred to the straightforward and uncomplicated principles of Charlie Oakshott.

Irene Chancellor broke in on her companion's thoughts again: 'Well, since you're away tomorrow, and I am not likely to see you again for heaven knows when, you had better come round tonight for supper *à deux* – yes?'

THREE

Nothing changes, thought Oakshott, remembering a time, not all that long past, when he had crossed Whitehall in just such a snowstorm: the evening of his fateful encounter with his brother's estranged wife Harriet. The reflection caused him to pause in the middle of the street, the momentary lapse of concentration to win him a curse from a passing brewer's drayman who nearly ran him over.

A sullen log fire guttered in the main hall of Admiralty, and a small group of naval officers were warming their backsides before it while they awaited a summons to whatever business had brought them there. Oakshott joined them, and watched with some interest to see his soaked boat cloak begin to steam. He had left a chitty stating his name and business with the doorkeeper; he was not kept waiting for long.

'This way, Captain Oakshott, sir.'

Up uncarpeted staircases and along dimly-lit corridors, he followed his guide. A tap on an oaken door. A call to enter.

The office was small, and furnished with a desk and chair, a chair for a visitor, and a dark portrait of some long-forgotten admiral glowering above the overmantle of a quite lively coal fire. Oakshott felt warm for the first time since alighting from the stuffy, overcrowded stagecoach that had delivered him at the George Inn, Southwark.

'Lord Charles – it has been a long time. How are you, sir?' A wizened little mannikin in seedy black rose from behind the desk upon his entrance and extended a hand.

'Mr Manthorpe – how nice. How are you, sir?' Oakshott's natural flair for remembering names and faces had been well practised in a profession which provided a constant gamut of shipmates, friends, casual acquaintances, loved ones and bitter enemies. 'Plymouth in 'ninety-three, was it not? And now you've been shifted to Admiralty.'

The other made a self-deprecating gesture. 'Now First Secretary of the Security Division,' he said.

'Ah, if I had known it was you who summoned me . . .' Oakshott left the rest unspoken.

'Yes,' said Manthorpe, 'I was not greatly pleased by the tone of my clerk's letter to you. My apologies. I was absent sick at the time. However –' the amiable, simian-like countenance grew suddenly grave '– the matter at issue is sufficiently – ah – *disturbing* to have put him rather more sharply on his mettle than his position warrants.'

'Oh,' said Oakshott, and took the seat that was indicated for him. 'Is it, now?'

'Would you care for a drop of brandy, Lord Charles?' asked the little man, delving into a drawer and producing a bottle and two rummers. 'At this hour, I usually partake. And not merely for medicinal reasons.'

'With much pleasure,' said Oakshott. 'And thank you.'

The glasses filled, pledges for the king, for victory over the wicked French having been exchanged, Manthorpe brought matters swiftly to a point.

'To facilitate the argument, Lord Charles,' he said, 'may I elicit your responses to a short list of questions?'

'Of course, Mr Manthorpe,' replied Oakshott, puzzled.

'I may – indeed, I must – add that your answers may form your defence at a future court martial,' said the mannikin who, having put on a pair of spectacles and taken up a sheet of paper, was eyeing his companion over the lenses.

'Will they, now?' responded Oakshott. 'Well, pray continue, sir.'

'I cast your mind back to the fifteenth December of last

year,' said Manthorpe, referring to his paper. 'You were aboard *Javelin*, shaping course for England. Cape Trafalgar – do I have the name right? – was abeam . . .

'*What* did you say, Lord Charles?'

'Nothing,' said Oakshott.

'You encountered there a Danish convoy, and . . .'

'And I fired upon one of the escorts, bringing down her mizzen topgallant,' supplied Oakshott. 'And this in response to the Dane having fired upon one of our patrol vessels. So it is for this that I am to be court martialled, hey, Mr Manthorpe?'

'And with your leave, Captain Oakshott,' murmured Manthorpe, with a keen glance over the top of his spectacles, 'I will continue the questions.'

Oakshott nodded. Glowered. Sank back in his seat.

'You boarded the leader of the Danish escorts,' said the other, 'the one you had fired upon. Certain discussions took place. What was the outcome of these discussions?'

'That I ordered the Danish captain, upon his parole, to put the convoy into Gibraltar and submit to a thorough search for contraband,' replied Oakshott.

Manthorpe nodded. 'And the Danish captain – he gave you verbal agreement to this order – as one officer to another?'

'Not precisely,' said Oakshott. 'This fellow – Lieutenant Lehmann was his name, as I recall – didn't speak a word of the king's English. The transaction was carried out through an intermediary. A third party who was voyaging aboard the Dane.'

A sharp glance from Manthorpe. 'The name of this – *intermediary*, Captain?'

'Mmm – Bernstorff. Count Axel Bernstorff.'

'Bernstorff – aah!'

Oakshott thought he discerned the beginnings of a smile at the corners of the other's exceedingly mobile, simian lips – as Manthorpe made a pencilled notation upon his sheet of paper. Having done this, the Admiralty secretary took up another sheet.

'I have now, Captain,' he said, 'to read to you the – necessarily – abridged contents of a report which has reached us from our intelligence contacts in the French port of Toulon, which unhappy place is known to you, I think?'

'You could say – intimately,' responded Oakshott with feeling.*

'This report, which, for reasons you will appreciate, has taken some considerable time to reach us,' said Manthorpe, 'tells of a convoy of escorted Danish merchantmen that put into Toulon some four weeks after encountering you off Cape Trafalgar. The convoy had not – as you had supposed – put into Gibraltar to be searched.'

'Had it not, by God?' cried Oakshott, much put about by this intelligence and its sinister implications.

'In Toulon, the Danes discharged their cargo,' resumed the secretary. 'For reasons of secrecy that you will appreciate, I will not particularize the actual nature of the cargo. Suffice to say that it was positively and irremediably contraband material from the Baltic, augmented by other material likely to be of aid to His Majesty's enemies – and the latter cargo had been taken aboard in various ports of the North African littoral *after* the convoy passed through the Straits of Gibraltar.'

'That bastard!' exclaimed Oakshott, and drove a fist into the palm of the other hand. 'That double-dealing, foppish bastard!'

'You are perhaps referring to Count Bernstorff, Lord Charles?' was the other's mildly inflected inquiry.

'Dammit, yes, I am,' growled Oakshott.

'Bernstorff is known to us,' said Manthorpe. 'He is – frankly – a spy. Nor is money the inducement. He simply

*For an account of Oakshott's part in the fateful siege of Toulon please refer to *Run Out the Guns* (Century 1984)

does it for the sense of power that the occupation provides for his curious temperament. Half Swedish, half Italian, so I believe. In any event, the ethnic mixture is suitably exotic and volatile for one of his chosen calling. Yes, I would say that you were badly gulled by Bernstorff, Lord Charles. And that, in the present promising state of your career, could be fatal. I am very sorry.' And he looked sorry.

'It will come to a court martial?' asked Oakshott, knowing the answer full well; for much lesser faults than this, he had heard tell of captains – brilliant careerists all, and marked for admiralcy – who had been put on the beach, their advancements limited to derisory appointments in the dockyards and such.

'It may come to it,' said Manthorpe. 'Especially since the dossier on the case is being forwarded to the Prime Minister.'

'Then I'm surely done for,' said Oakshott. 'But, tell me, Mr Manthorpe – how is it that you came to learn of the parole issue? Surely Bernstorff did not bruit it around Toulon.'

'He may, or may not have,' responded the other. 'In the event, Lieutenant Jakeman of *Mole* put in a report about your action. Without that, quite frankly, I might have contrived to hush up the matter. As it is . . .' He spread his hands in a gesture of helplessness. 'Do you follow me?'

'I see it all,' said Oakshott.

It was still snowing when he left the building and, pulling up the collar of his cloak about his ears, went out to brave the blizzard of Whitehall and the Strand.

His footsteps directed him towards Mogg's Diversions, that early precursor of the music hall where once his sister-in-law Harriet had worked as a singer. This singularly genteel establishment was crowded as usual, and Oakshott opted to stand at the semi-circular serving counter at the rear of the auditorium, where he called for a glass of hot rum punch and idly watched the clientele and the entertainment on the apron stage – and all the while his gloomy thoughts turned to his present, potentially ruinous situation.

The fiat would go out from the Prime Minister's office that Captain Oakshott was to be court-martialled and an example made of him to encourage the other captains of the fleet to take more seriously the 'Stop and Search' policy that was putting Britain and the Baltic states more at loggerheads by the hour, and might even end by throwing the latter into the arms of Bonaparte and the French.

Well, he thought, Charlie Oakshott was unlikely to be still at sea when the war extended to the Baltic; this first year of the nineteenth century would see him on the beach for sure. He took a long pull of the spiced punch.

It was then, over the rim of his rummer, that he observed himself being watched, and by a woman. Not to put too fine a point on it, a lady. She was seated alone in one of the boxes at the side of the stage, and was masked in the Venetian fashion, white-faced in kid-leather. Her hair was superbly dressed and powdered. She wore a gown of sprigged silk, cut after the French mode in imitation of the Greek. And she was most discernibly looking towards the tall figure lolling against the serving counter – not that this was a matter for comment: the Royal Navy had been elevated to a supremely high regard in the eyes of their countrymen, particularly after the Nile, and Oakshott was used to being stared at, smiled at and leered at, when in uniform.

The stage having now been filled with a chorus of ladies and gentlemen, the orchestra struck up the air of a cantata which had first been performed in Naples following Nelson's victory and had been well-received before the king and the royal family at Windsor in the previous summer:

'Long live the British Hero!
Long live great Nelson!

It is he who drove far from us all affliction.
It is he who gave peace to our troubled hearts.'

Oakshott, who was tone deaf as near as makes no odds, was nevertheless sufficiently taken by the excellent sentiments of the libretto that he let his attention stray from the lady in the box till the cantata was concluded. When next he glanced across towards her, he experienced a distinct livening of interest to see that she was still looking towards him; indeed, she was very pointedly using a quizzing glass. And the Venetian mask, that only hid the features from brow to nose, revealed that she was *smiling* . . .

Out pistols and cutlasses! Stand by to board!

Mogg's Diversions, despite its impeccable reputation for probity, was known to attract a few ladies of the night – but always those of the very highest, most discreet and expensive sort. Add to that, certain ladies of quality – taken, no doubt, by the new spirit abroad that the Age of Reason, the American and French revolutions had engendered – often were to be seen there, alone, or with another female friend, and invariably masked after the Venetian manner.

Oakshott ordered of the serving wench another bumper of rum punch, which he swallowed down in swift order.

Well, then, Charlie, he told himself. Let's cap this disastrous day with what my poor dead brother Jack would have fancifully termed a tilt at the lists of Hymen.

Oakshott set the rummer down upon the counter, carefully adjusted his stock, and turned round to begin his assault.

The box was empty; the masked lady had gone.

Alone, his hopes of a conquest dashed, he paid his score and went out into the night, turning his footsteps towards Covent Garden, where he knew of several good lodging houses. A combination of drink, the rapid change from the warmth of Mogg's to the arctic night without, coupled with a nagging depression of spirits, had so dulled Oakshott's keen sense of direction that he had not taken more than a couple of turns uphill from the Strand before he found himself quite lost in the labyrinth of narrow alleyways that surrounded the environs of the garden. He was addressing himself to the relatively simple task of determining north from south with the aid of the galaxy of stars that shone beneficently down from the now cloudless sky, when he became aware that he was being followed.

The dark figure was cloaked and hooded, and regarding him from the corner of an alleyway half a pistol shot to the rear. As Oakshott turned – having experienced very forcibly that sixth sense of being watched – the figure drew back out of sight.

Oakshott was not greatly put out. The day of the savage Mohocks was gone. It would be a brave, not to say unpatriotic, cutpurse who would chance his arm against a six-foot naval officer. He waited a few moments in case the watcher reappeared – and then went on his way.

But not for long . . .

Having oriented himself by the stars, Oakshott crossed the street to turn up an alleyway that must inevitably lead to St Paul's church. In so doing he glimpsed the cloaked figure – closer to him now – darting back into the shadows.

'You there!' bawled Oakshott in the voice that he had fine-honed and modulated so as to carry from quarter-deck to masthead in a south-wester, 'What the devil are you at? Come out and declare yourself!'

No sign or response resulting from his challenge, Oakshott moved swiftly towards the spot where his mystery follower had disappeared. With no more than a slight irritation coupled with an understandable curiosity, he determined to confront the other and, if necessary, teach him a lesson. Reaching the corner of an alleyway, he was interested to see that his quarry had left footprints in the ankle-deep snow. They led off into the dark maw of the alley.

Curiosity fought, in Oakshott's strictly logical mind, with a disinclination to waste time on a fruitless pursuit. And curiosity won. Prudently wrapping the tail of his cloak round his left forearm so as to parry a possible knife slash, he marched swiftly up the alley in the footsteps of the stranger.

Having progressed about as far as a good hand can throw a heaving line in still air, he paused to listen. In doing so he stirred his quarry, who must have been lying low a short distance ahead. There was a sudden flurry of footfalls in deep snow, the sound of laboured breathing. The game was afoot. Oakshott gave chase. It was heavy going through the snow, which had drifted deeply in the dark canyon of the alley. The moon was down and ahead was all blackness; no sign of the other man, though his footprints were starkly visible against the virgin snow, and widely spaced with a lot of powdering; so the fellow must be moving at a fair rate of knots, thought Oakshott.

And then, with the dramatic finality of a slammed door, there appeared before him a high wall – ten feet high at least was his first summation – which completely blanked off the end of the alley. No through road.

'Well, I'm damned!' breathed Oakshott aloud. 'The fellow – whoever he is – must be an acrobat!'

There was clear evidence of the manner of his quarry's escape. First, a termination of the footprints at the base of the wall; next, a certain amount of scuffling, as might be caused by a man gathering himself up, shifting his stance and so forth, for a prodigious leap; and then – looking up – Oakshott was able to see, clearly etched against the night sky, the dip in the white crest of snow on the top of the wall where the stranger had completed his leap, held hard with both hands, and vaulted himself over.

Oakshott shook his head in wonderment.

'I don't know of a man alive who could perform a standing

leap to that height,' he mused. 'And there's one who *certainly* can't. And that's Charlie Oakshott.'

He turned about and went back the way he had come.

After a restless night in a tolerable enough boarding house, Oakshott breakfasted off a round of grilled ham and eggs, a pint of ale; then took post down to Beaulieu River, Hampshire, where lay Buckler's Hard, that most remarkable shipbuilding enterprise of the time; where Albion's wooden walls, wrought from the great belt of oak forests which spanned southern England from west to east, went down Buckler's slipways and became, all in their turn, the far-off storm-tossed ships that held the line.

Oakshott's first view, upon alighting from the fly which had brought him from the posting inn at Beaulieu, was of his own ship lying up on the top of a slipway, her weight supported on her keel by baulks of timber propped against the rubbing strake. Sheerlegs loomed like stick insects over the stub of her mainmast. And to Oakshott's nostrils there came the familiar dockyard reek – indefinably pleasant – of hot iron and charred wood.

There she lies, he told himself. All of her, bared as a bride to her groom; like as not, he would never again know the fierce delight of piling canvas atop of her and driving her sharp stem through the blue water; nor command her 16-gun broadsides against the French and win a certain glory. He sighed, picked up his valise, nodded to the driver to follow after with his sea chest, and went to rejoin his command – for how long, he had no notion.

The officer of the day had espied his captain from afar. Pipes were shrilling through the ship to call the duty watch and quartermasters on deck. A veritable cacophony greeted his march over the brow and on to the quarter-deck. First Lieutenant Tom Brewster was there to greet him with a salute and to take his proffered hand.

'Welcome back aboard, sir,' said the American.

'Thank you, Number One,' responded Oakshott, and, observing the other more closely, was constrained to add: 'What – have you had an altercation with a slammed door –or did someone tap your claret?'

Brewster had a considerable black eye, and his prominently aquiline nose was swollen and reddened.

'I have had – um – a little trouble ashore, sir,' he responded – with a savage, sidelong glance to the midshipman of the watch and the chief quartermaster, who were with difficulty suppressing broad grins. 'But I would prefer to discuss it with you later – sir.'

Oakshott nodded. 'How goes the refit?' he asked.

Brewster seemed glad to change the subject from the matter of his damaged appearance. Directing his captain's attention towards the stump of the mainmast, he walked him away from the group on the quarter-deck, talking all the time.

'It's a topsy-turvy world, sir,' he opined. 'The teak, which was promised in five weeks, was delivered in one, and the decks, as you will see, are all marvellously well relaid. On the other hand, the mainmast, which should have been renewed in no time at all, still awaits the arrival of the topmast and topgallant.

'Mr Adams – Mr *Henry* Adams' – at this, the American rolled his eyes towards a very fine, solid house nearby, at the edge of the river – 'Mr Adams informs me that he will flay the hide off his chief shipwright's back if the mainmast is not up, and we not back in the water by Thursday. But I would not go banco on it.'

Oakshott grinned. As a very small and junior midshipman, he had early made the acquaintance of the legendary Henry Adams, former overseer of the King's Yard, Deptford, who had later become a freelance and, taking on the lease of the private Buckler's Hard, had secured contracts from the navy to build some of the finest warships afloat.

Adams was – by any yardstick – a character . . .

Oakshott remembered how, when ashore in the dockyard on some trivial errand relating to navigational equipment or somesuch, he had been accosted by a gentleman who seemed to him of most impossibly advanced age.

Said the gentleman: 'Do you know me, boy?'

'Nu-no, sir,' piped the young Oakshott.

'Well, I am not God, boy,' came the response. 'But you may regard me' – and here the wrinkled countenance was brought so close to the boy midshipman's face that he caught the fresh tang of peppermint on the other's breath – 'but you may regard me as God – *locally!*'

So saying, he held out a carved ivory comfit box.

'Have a peppermint, you poor deprived child,' said the god of Buckler's Hard.

'There is a dispatch for you, sir,' said Pepe Lopez. 'From Admiralty. Arrived yesterday, by hand of officer.'

They were in the stern cabin – Oakshott, Brewster and Lopez. *Javelin*'s captain had called for his steward Bantock to open a bottle of his prized claret, to celebrate his return and to drive out the cold.

'You had a pleasant furlough, sir?' asked the captain's secretary.

'Well enough,' replied Oakshott, pledging both his companions with a raised glass. 'I married off my sister-in-law to a very agreeable gentleman who will – or so I trust – take the burden of my family estate from off my back, and gently deposit the same upon my brother's heir when he comes of age. So the weeks away cannot be said to have been wasted.'

Lopez's discerning dark eyes may or may not have perceived the shadow of conflict that coloured his captain's expression when Oakshott delivered the flippant response. He merely passed over the dispatch in question, which was a four-folded sheet of parchment sealed with the Admiralty crown.

Oakshott broke the seal, begged pardon of his companions, and moved over to the light of the stern windows, the better to read the missive.

(It's a summons to my court martial. Pitt's hand was swift. I shall be bidden to hand over the command to my Number One and present myself at a time and place herein inscribed, there to answer the charges laid against me . . .)

The dispatch, in fact, was a horse of an entirely different colour. It was dated a week previously – predating his interview with Mr Manthorpe – and couched in a decidedly encouraging vein:

> Capt Ld Chas Oakshott RN
> HMS *Javelin*
> By Hand of Officer
>
> Sir,
>
> You are commanded by Their Lordships to proceed upon completion of your refit to Harwich, and there to put yourself under the orders of Commdr Sir Jas Freakley, carrying his broad pennant in HMS *Jaunty*, for service in the German Ocean and the approaches to the Baltic . . .

The letter was signed by a senior clerk unknown to Oakshott, and this functionary, surely, had not been apprised of Oakshott's present, parlous condition; nor would the department of Admiralty responsible for postings have moved a ship and her captain to a war command when the latter was under dire threat of court martial.

With a bit of luck, thought Oakshott, he might reach Harwich and get himself lost in the wide expanse of the German Ocean while the whole business of the Danes blew over. Thank heaven that the organization in the Admiralty was not equal to letting one hand know what the other was doing. Ever optimistic, Oakshott's spirits rose like a lark.

'Number One,' he said, turning, 'Mr Adams faithfully promises that the mainmast will be complete on Thursday – do I have it right?'

'Thursday for sure, sir,' confirmed the American.

'And what time is high tide on Thursday eve?'

Brewster screwed up his lean countenance in the effort of a minor piece of mental arithmetic. 'It has to be no later than nine p.m., sir,' he said at length. 'And the moon will be up.'

'Then have the ship in all respects ready for sea when the last of Mr Adams's dockyard mateys goes over the side, Number One,' said Oakshott. 'And be prepared to slip at high tide and proceed to sea on the ebb.'

The American grinned. 'So we're under orders then, sir?' he asked.

Oakshott passed him the Admiralty dispatch. 'You read it too, Pepe,' he said. 'And acknowledge receipt to Admiralty.

'Now – let us kill this bottle of excellent claret, gentlemen, and drink another to our new enterprise.'

'Commodore Freakley, I know,' said Brewster. 'We were under his broad pennant in *Leander* at Tenerife.'

'I've never come across him,' said Oakshott.

'Disciplinarian of the old school,' supplied Brewster. 'Though not a hanger and flogger. You and Sir James will get along fine, sir, for he's a gentleman through and through. A three-bottle man and a very keen rider to hounds. They call him Lucky Jimmy, for he succeeded to the baronetcy after a whole crew of cousins dropped off the hook. Next, he married a wealthy widow and came into enough properties in East Anglia as provide him with a different mansion to live in every day of the week. This really is a most tolerable claret, ain't it, Pepe?'

The three men seated round the long table that stood athwart the stern cabin were well into their cups, and much improved by the same. Oakshott, who was arguably the hardest-headed of the three, now that he thought he saw the sword of Damocles, if not removed from above his head, at least suspended on a thicker piece of line, found himself embarking upon a mildly philosophical contemplation of his companions . . .

That Brewster, he thought, now what is it that brings a fellow like him – a man of means and with some education – to cut ties with his own country and serve a king and country that his own folk had rejected by force of arms? A scented fop, he scarcely fitted the image of the Yankee frontiersman. As for his dress! – a regular Macaroni, he, and right out of the song. No oblique hints had been able to persuade Brewster that the navy's regulation blue coat, though it might allow of subtle differencing as regards cut and decoration, should not be of watered silk; nor should the cocked hat be embellished with a riot of assorted plumes, and one added every year for luck.

Brewster had pledged himself to become one of the first admirals of the first-class American navy-to-be, and there was no doubt but that the Yankees would find in him a damned fine admiral if ever that unlikely force were ever to come into being – for as an all-round officer and a Number One there were none better.

Which brought Oakshott to Pepe Lopez . . .

Discernibly drunk, now, with those shrewd and berry-black eyes hooded and seemingly sleepy, there was no doubt that, put to it, he could still play three simultaneous games of chess – as he had done many times during the commission – and win all with ease against the best players in the ship – Oakshott included. But Pepe was talking now, and he had not been listening . . .

'I have been a subscriber to *The Times* since I took up employment with the navy,' said the Spanish Moor, his precise articulation giving the lie to his heavy-lidded eyes, 'and the London *Times* is much opposed to the theory and practice of our – that is to say, Mr Pitt's – policy towards the Armed Neutrality. The editor, Mr John Walter, is of the opinion that the Russian Tsar Paul – who is insane – will be driven to making common cause with Bonaparte and bring all the Baltic states into the war against us. That is what Mr Walter thinks.

'What do you think, Captain?' he added.

'For my part,' responded the other, 'and speaking plainly, I see no point in shilly-shally. If the Danes and others want to support Bonaparte to the tune of supplying him with war materials, then let 'em nail their colours to the mast and fight for their seamy trade. I tell you, gentlemen, we aboard this ship have been witness to the double dealing that lies behind the hypocrisy of the Armed Neutrality, which is no neutrality, but merely a contrivance to get the best out of both worlds – grab at the spoils of war without getting your hands dirty. That's what I think.'

Pepe nodded. If he considered his captain's view to be simplistic, if not intemperate, he did not show it; instead, the clever eyes narrowed with keen interest.

'You say, sir, that we have been witness – do you refer to the incident of the *Hedeby*?' he asked. 'Do you perhaps have further intelligence of that affair?'

'I do,' said Oakshott.

And he told them of the Admiralty summons to London, and all that had transpired from it.

'You were right about Bernstorff, Pepe,' said Oakshott with commendable grace, 'and I was wrong. The fellow's a bad 'un, and known as such to our people. I should have marked him down by the cut of his jib. But I tell you – if ever our paths cross again, it will be pistols for two at dawn and breakfast for one.'

'And will this court-martial threat come to aught, sir?' asked Brewster.

'I see no impediment to it,' replied Oakshott. 'Save putting as much blue water as possible 'twixt me and the Judge Advocate General of the Fleet.' He eyed the others and grinned.

'I will call upon Mr Henry Adams first thing in the morning, sir,' said Brewster. 'And I'll hope to persuade him to have his men work overnight on Wednesday by torchlight, so that we can make the midday tide on Thursday.'

'That's the ticket, Number One,' said Oakshott, taking up the fourth bottle of claret which Bantock had just brought in on soft-footed tread. 'Here's to deep water.

'And now, Number One,' he added. 'You must tell us how you came about that shiner and bloody nose.'

'It was brought about,' said Brewster, 'when I went to a fair near Beaulieu. Now, this was not a fair as I know a fair, as my folks know a fair in the country towns of Massachusetts. Not being over familiar with English customs, I had never heard of what is known over here as a hiring fair – that's to say where men and boys, women and girls, offer their labour in the fields and in the farmhouses for an agreed sum per annum.

'Then, gentlemen, I saw me this most pulchritudinous wench offering herself as an upstairs maid – whatever *that* might be, I asked myself – for a measly fifteen guineas per annum. So I bid for this maid, and had her for fifteen, which I thought was cheap at the price for the time I should be at Buckler's Hard.

'You laugh, gentlemen – but one should not mock the ignorant.

'Explaining to her – her name is Dimity – that I should not be hereabouts for many more weeks, I pointed out that she could keep the unexpired portion of the fifteen guineas when I had gone.

'I will pause awhile till you shall have purged your mirth, gentlemen.'

'I'm most awfully sorry, Number One,' said Oakshott. 'Do continue.'

'Thank you, sir. Thank you, secretary. Yes, we spent a most pleasant day together, ending in a protracted walk along the strand, where I instructed Dimity in the habits of the marsh bittern and other wild birds. Later, we enjoyed an excellent veal and ham supper at a local hostelry.

'It was when we were coming back in the direction of Buckler's Hard that these two dark-avised and brawny fellows accosted the pair of us, Dimity and me. Announcing themselves as the wench's brothers, they demanded to know the address at which I should be employing their sister. I was only able to answer HMS *Javelin*, which, though a king's ship of war, was not an address that appeared to commend itself to these fellows in any high regard.

'It was then that they fell upon me – with the results you see.'

This airy tale, lightly recounted, had the effect of raising Oakshott's spirits the more.

'Well, you learned your lesson, Number One,' he declared. 'And you will be more careful next time you buy a piglet in a poke. Seriously, my dear fellow, I never saw any advancement or profit in an officer keeping a woman aboard. It invariably causes dissension on the lower deck and rivalry in the wardroom. You are well shut of your Dimity.'

'Not so, sir,' retorted the American. 'I am by no means shut of her.'

'Don't tell me that!'

'Sir,' cried the American, 'has she not been calling at Buckler's Hard every day since, and imploring me to take her for a walk down the strand? – despite those lubberly brothers!'

'With a veal and ham supper thrown in for good measure, after the lesson in – *ornithology*, Number One?' asked Pepe Lopez, smiling down into his glass.

The American threw him a look of mild loathing.

'Well, Number One, you have as good a reason as I to make the noon tide on Thursday,' opined Oakshott.

Mr Henry Adams was all Wednesday night in the flare of torchlight, supervising his shipwrights stepping the topmast and topgallant upon *Javelin*'s main and setting up the spars, the standing and the running rigging.

Oakshott, who had stayed awake all night watching the work from his poop deck, had not approached the lessee of Buckler's Hard all that time, for reasons that he never could have explained even to himself. In the dawn light, Adams's face, which seemed in the years between their last and only other meeting, to have become much younger, had taken on the sort of pinch-cheeked tiredness that one sees in representations of martyred saints.

By dawn, in the event, *Javelin* was ready to be slipped.

Oakshott went up to the genius of Buckler's Hard and proffered his hand.

'Mr Adams, I am most grateful for your excellent service,' he said. 'Will you take breakfast with me?'

The other's wrinkled countenance was expressionless, like a slate upon which one could write one's own message.

'Ah! – Midshipman Oakshott!' he declared.

'Formerly,' grinned the other.

'I remember you well,' said Adams, 'and marked you in my mind for advancement. I remember with what disdain you scorned my condescension and told me – silently, but in so many words – what I could do with my peppermints.'

They both laughed.

While Oakshott and Adams were enjoying steward Bantock's excellent breakfast of his captain's favourite fried eggs on oatcakes, First Lieutenant Brewster was watching over the loading of stores, this being more convenient when the ship was high and dry on the slipway, and tending to give her more 'bottom' when she went down to kiss water.

'Haul away handsomely!'

'Check her!'

'Lower away!'

Piece by piece, they came aboard and were stowed below: the victuals of hard tack and salt meat; lime juice against the scurvy; hogsheads of rum: roundshot for the guns, with faggot, grape, bar and chain shot – everything in its place. Last of all came the *raison d'être* for the sleek, deep-water frigate: the casks of black powder that would propel those shapes of iron through wooden walls and the bodies of men.

'Provisioning completed, sir.' Brewster presented himself in the stern cabin, his grossly plumed hat tucked under his arm.

'Up to standard, Number One,' said Oakshott, glancing at his half-hunter which lay open on the table top by his plate. 'And it only lacks an hour and five minutes to high tide. Mr Adams and I had decided that it was not too early to round off breakfast with a bumper of sherry wine – the consignment we picked up in Algeciras, you will remember. Will you join us?'

'With much pleasure, sir.' Brewster took his place at the table.

'As I was saying to Mr Adams, a good refit, Number One,' said Oakshott. 'And smartly completed. With luck, we shall be moving off down the Solent within a couple of hours.

'Have there been any deliveries of dispatches aboard, Number One,' he asked, 'since I left the upper deck?'

Brewster raised a comprehending eyebrow. 'No, sir,' he murmured.

'Well, then,' said Oakshott, 'let us enjoy our sherry, then set about slipping, Your health, Mr Adams.'

Javelin's captain had scarcely pledged the genius of Buckler's Hard when there came a tap on the cabin door and the duty midshipman entered – a pale-faced child of thirteen.

'Captain, sir!' piped the lad.

'What is it, Mr Willis?' asked Oakshott.

'Dispatch for you, sir.'

'Ah – thank you, Mr Willis.'

Oakshott took the missive, noted that it carried the Admiralty symbol of a foul anchor and was heavily sealed. He weighed it in his hand for a few moments – and also in his conscience. This might well – almost certainly would – bear a summons which would require him to hand over his command to the next most senior officer, Brewster, and repair to London, or wherever, to face his court martial.

He was aware that Brewster's eye was covertly upon him; Mr Adams was busily enjoying his sherry, rolling it round his mouth most appreciatively; Oakshott took his cue from the latter.

'Yes, a robust little wine, Mr Adams,' he said. 'Will you do me the honour of accepting a case in thanks for your splendid work on *Javelin*?'

'Most kind of you, sir,' responded the other. 'Very many thanks, and with much pleasure.'

'See to it, please, Bantock,' said Oakshott.

And he put the Admiralty dispatch into his coat-tail pocket, unopened.

The slipping went well at high tide, with never the hint of a hitch. After *Javelin* had slid easily down the greased slipway, she wallowed gently in three fathoms offshore while the men who had worked on her waved and cheered from the hard and wished the crew fair winds and safe havens, pledging them in strong ale. Two beetle-browed individuals stood out from the rest of the spectators and did not wave and cheer for the men on the crowded decks of the slender frigate. A few paces from these two individuals, a young girl of some considerable pulchritude – to employ Thomas A. Brewster's term – wept into her handkerchief.

'Make all plain sail, Number One,' said Oakshott.

'Aye, *aye*, sir!' was the other's fervent response, with a glance towards the two brothers on the hard; he gave another, more tender glance at the girl he had left behind him.

'Steady as you go.'

'Steady it is, sir.'

'I'll have a two-gun salute to amuse the populace.'

'Aye, aye, sir. Two-gun salute.'

As the frigate took the wind and nosed swiftly out of the Beaulieu River on the fast-flowing ebb, the sharp crack of a 24-pounder shattered the stillness, echoed and re-echoed from the wooded slopes surrounding, and brought half the birds in Hampshire, surely, on the wing and screeching. The shot was followed by another.

The white powder smoke hung low over the water, drifting along on the wind at the same speed as the frigate, part hiding her from the folks ashore. But crewmen and dockyard mateys – and certainly one tearful young girl – kept waving till *Javelin* was out of sight.

'Call me when Needs Ore Point is abeam,' said Oakshott, swinging down the companionway.

'Aye, aye, sir, Needs Ore Point,' responded Brewster. The American's eyes followed the captain till the other's cocked hat dipped below the deck.

And now he's going to open that damned dispatch, thought the first lieutenant. Do I hope that it's a recall? And if it is, the captain won't be able to disobey, for it's certain that a copy will have been sent to Lucky Jimmy in Harwich.

Do I want to be captain of *Javelin* for so long as it takes for them to send another to rule over me? I think not.

I think I'd sooner stay with Charlie Oakshott . . .

Down below, Oakshott made a great play of delaying the

ordeal of opening the dispatch; first pouring himself another glass of sherry, next tapping the barometer, then looking out the side windows to ensure himself that the ship was on course in the deep channel, which veered to the starboard side on that particular stretch of the estuary.

Finally, when there was nothing left but for him to address himself to the distasteful task, he broke the seal and read the contents, which came to him, at first scanning, only in brief snatches; like the recollection of one of those old songs of the sea that put one in mind of a permanence of loyalty, comradeship and a power above oneself.

. . . in view of which, Their Lordships require me to inform you that no further action will be taken . . . the matter of the *Hedeby* incident is shelved . . . will not be held to the demerit of your career . . .

Through eyes glazed over with tears of relief and release, he read a footnote scribbled in pencil and signed by his good old acquaintance, Chief Secretary Manthorpe:

> I am not empowered to advise you how this strange turn of events came about, Lord Charles. Suffice to say that you have powerful friends in most unexpectedly high places.

To his surprise, the reading of the missive, the preliminaries, and his emotional reactions had taken far longer than he would have believed. In no time at all, the midshipman of the watch came down to inform him that the point was abeam. Oakshott clapped on his hat and followed the lad back up top.

Part Two

TO THE BALTIC

FOUR

'Masthead – deck! *Arrow*'s gone out of sight on the port quarter!'

At the hail from above, Oakshott strained his eyes into the murk of darkness and flying spray, looking to starboard where, every so often, when the ship rose on a wavecrest, he dimly discerned a flash of pale greyness that betokened a set of reefed sails, and occasionally the faint glint of his other consort's stern lantern.

'Nothing to port, Quartermaster,' he shouted across the heaving quarter-deck. '*Arrow* has lost us. See to it that we stay within sight of *Jaunty.*' The order was acknowledged by a wave.

Bantock appeared up top, carrying a mug of steaming cocoa. With a wild following sea as an impediment, it took him a while to proceed by hand-holds from the top of the companionway to the mizzen chains where Oakshott and Brewster clung. After Bantock came the American's devoted negro serving lad Cuthbert, also bearing cocoa for his master. The two officers took the steaming, rum-laced beverages gratefully and sucked them down.

'*Arrow* may find us again in the dawn, sir,' opined Brewster. 'It ain't like Cap'n Bolton to lose station – even in *this.*'

'This' was an equinoctial westerly gale which had hit the three British frigates sailing in company off the coast of Denmark that March night.

The present enterprise, the brainchild of Commodore

Lucky Jimmy Freakley, was a sweep in force intended to catch out any neutral vessels leaving the Baltic with contraband and attempting to make a French port or proceed on down to the Mediterranean. Sailing in sight of each other in line abreast, their intent was to comb a swath of sea forty miles wide in the approaches to the opening of the Skagerrak; back and forth, one hundred and forty miles each leg; close-hauled one way, running free the other, day and night.

The plan had sounded quite plausible, as delivered by Lucky Jimmy, during a sumptuous dinner of a baron of beef in the stern cabin of the leader's frigate in Harwich. Oakshott and Bolton, captains respectively of the two ships designated to sail with the commodore, had almost swallowed it whole. Even the part where the latter, slicing himself another thick haunch of succulent, underdone meat, had grinned a wild-eyed aside: 'What's more, gentlemen, there may be the concomitant advantage of encountering a damned Frenchie or two. Even a ship of the line, hey? What price the three of us cutting in and confounding some Frog sixty-four, and he all unawares with his washing on the line and all hands below, hey?' The baronet's zany, high-coloured countenance took on the expression of the zealot as he pressed into service mustard and pepper pots, salt and vinegar, and proceeded to demonstrate to his subordinates how three skilfully handled frigates – employing the tactics of three mastiffs tackling a bull, one cutting in for a slash of fangs to the throat whilst his consorts go for the unguarded belly – may overcome the mightier opponent by speed, courage and concerted action.

'Concerted action, gentlemen – that's the ticket!' had been Commodore Sir James Freakley's summation. After which he sat back and washed down his beef with a bumper of claret. And his subordinates exchanged glances and smiled thinly in response.

He has the right touch of boldness, thought Oakshott at

the time. Though there's never been a successful frigate action against a battleship in my recollection, and certainly not in this war. As to the venue – we've no charts of the Skagerrak as would give safe passage close inshore to a herring boat. And if the prevailing westerlies should veer to the north, we'd be on a lee shore . . .

Oakshott, who had spent some months scouring the coast of the Low Countries as far as the Baltic approaches, at his own expense when on half pay before the war, had had these reservations about the enterprise, but had held his peace. After all, he reasoned, the commodore wasn't given the nickname of Lucky Jimmy for nothing.

Oakshott was later to call himself to account for not expressing the doubts that were raised in his mind on that occasion.

'It's worsening!' opined Brewster. 'We're near the eye of the storm!'

The observation need scarcely to have been made. Running free with the mizzen bare and only rags of canvas for'ard, the ship was plunging like a steeplechaser over ploughland, driving her nose deeply after every leap and fetching up cascades of white water as far aft as the quarter-deck, which in its turn was being pooped by the following seas with every third breaker. Scarcely had the words left the American's lips when the graceful bowsprit was plucked from its seating and carried away into the darkness ahead, jibs and all – like a line of washing.

'Watch your helm!' cried Oakshott as *Javelin*, unbalanced by the loss of her headsails, began to pay off at the bow.

Fighting with the big double wheel, the quartermaster and his two assistants managed to hold the yawing somewhat in check, though the ship was now in the constant hazard of being broached to and rolled over on her beam ends.

It was then, in the immutable rule of the sea which says that when one thing goes amiss every other potential calamity will follow in train, that Ship's Carpenter Henshawe came up on deck to inform his captain that the Cole's chain pump had packed up: nothing that a couple of hours' work wouldn't put to rights, but meanwhile so much sea was coming inboard that the bilges were overflowing and the lower deck awash with hammocks, messdeck tables and other gear; in answer to which information, Oakshott nodded, bade Henshawe to carry on and do his best, jammed his hat more firmly down over his brow, and waited for the next inevitable figure in that dance of disasters. He had not long to wait.

'Masthead – deck! *Jaunty*'s mainmast is gone!'

Clinging to the mizzen chains, Oakshott brought his telescope to bear, one-handed. In all the wild pitching, he contrived to get a few brief glimpses of his leader, and it seemed to him that the glint of grey sail had somewhat diminished.

It was then that a pair of white rockets rose from the other ship.

'*Jaunty*'s signalling to anchor, sir.'

Oakshott snapped his telescope shut against his hip and tucked it into his belt. So – the old man had some intelligence of the depth of water. Maybe he had managed to take soundings – in which case his leadsmen were uncommonly skilled. Or he might have got a fix on the shore. Or maybe, like late Aunt Maude, he was an adept at reading tea leaves.

'Prepare to anchor!' shouted Oakshott.

The best bower anchor slipped into the white water as – gauging the moment to a smidgen – Oakshott ordered the ship to be brought about on the crest of a long, high wave. Assisted by a hastily unfurled mizzen, *Javelin* responded speedily to face wind and sea, and with scarce a roll on the way round.

There was a certain confusion for'ard, but presently the fo'c's'le officer came aft and reported that the anchor was holding – in five fathoms as near as he could determine.

'Very good, Mr Shacklock,' acknowledged Oakshott. 'Keep close anchor watch and report the slightest sign of dragging.'

'Aye, aye, sir.'

Resigning himself to a long night's vigil, Oakshott prudently went below, changed into dry clothes, had Bantock lash his wooden armchair to the foot of the quarter-deck companionway and took his place there, out of the wind and the spray, to await events.

As always, when all had been done that could be done, and the outcome reposed in the will of Fate, Oakshott enjoyed the ability to distance himself from the nagging doubts and fears of the present that bedevil lesser men. Instead, bracing his feet against the lower rung of the companionway to counteract the sickening fore and aft motion of *Javelin* springing on the weight of her anchor cable, he took from his breeches pocket the letter that had been delivered aboard on the morn of their departure from Harwich and re-read it for the umpteenth time with some pleasure. It was from his sister-in-law.

Dear Charlie,

It is with the greatest joy that I tell you the news that Dr Hodgkinson has informed me that I am to be brought to bed of child in the autumn. You will realize with what delight dearest Harry and I have this blessed intelligence & give thanks that little Charlie will no longer be the only child.

Things progress handsomely at Sennett. The new roof of the south wing is nearing completion and the stewpond has been drained and cleaned, to be restocked with carp. Harry –

ever indulgent – has told me that, after the baby has come, we must all to Bath.

How happy I am, Charlie dear, and how my only fears are for your safety. Though I know that the counsel will fall upon deaf ears, I beg you to take care . . .

So, Harriet was safely launched upon the sea of happy matrimony and continued motherhood. Oakshott relaxed in his armchair as well as the motion would allow him. He must have dozed off in fits and starts, for it seemed in no time at all that the midshipman of the watch came down to tell him that it was dawn, and *Jaunty* was in clear view, together with the Danish shore. Oakshott was up top in a trice.

There was no change in the state of the sea. The leader rose and fell over and over the wavecrests no more than five cables distant on the port hand. Beyond, a distant smudge of what looked like sand dunes marked a shoreline. So lucky Jimmy had sighted putty after all, thought Oakshott.

Jaunty had lost her mainmast right down to deck level, and rose and fell with a sullen sluggishness, taking in white water every time, which suggested that she was badly waterlogged. (On the credit side, Ship's Carpenter Henshawe was present to inform his captain that the pump was working again and they were making headway against the water below.) The visibility to seaward was no more than a mile at most. And the storm gave no sign of abating. So here we must stay, thought Oakshott, if nothing else intervenes, till she's blown herself out and I can escort the leader back to Harwich, happily on a capful of wind.

It was then that little Midshipman Cobbold, who was crouched up in the fore peak of the ship with a telescope trained on the leader, piped up in his high treble, which carried clearly downwind to the quarter-deck:

'*Jaunty*'s dragging her anchor – *fast!*'

Oakshott and the others grouped about him focused upon the leader, rising and falling half a mile away. Oakshott almost immediately discerned – as young Cobbold must have – that there was something that looked like a watchtower on the shore. And it was relative to this standing marker that *Jaunty* was clearly moving back downwind.

'She's on a soft bottom,' said Brewster at his ear. 'Sand, or clay, I shouldn't wonder. And if I ain't mistaken, the wind's veering.'

Oakshott had also become aware that, even since his arrival back on deck, the relative position of the other ship had changed, and that *Jaunty* was now abaft the beam. Nor was this due only to the fact that the other ship was dragging her anchor: another visual fix on the watchtower told him all he needed to know. The ship's stern was moving to point shorewards.

'You're right, Number One,' he shouted above the cry of the gale. 'The wind's shifting to the north. We're on a lee shore!'

'*Jaunty*'s being dragged on to the putty!'

Then came a hail from the masthead: '*Jaunty*'s signalling!'

A display of flags was seen to be streaming from the leader's fore topmast yard. The busy midshipmen strained their eyes to read the message and addressed themselves to the signal book.

'TAKE – ME – IN – TOW!'

'*Jaunty* requests to be taken in tow, sir!' cried the midshipmen almost in unison.

But Oakshott, anticipating the leader's demand, had already given the order to weigh anchor and make sail.

'Anchor's a'trip – up and down!'

Freed of the ground, *Javelin*'s head swung round to port.

'Steer for *Jaunty*!' shouted Oakshott. 'And I'll wear ship a cable short of her!'

'Aye, aye, sir!'

Unbidden, young Shacklock of the fo'c's'le party had already given the order to flake down the tow rope, laying out the coils of thick hemp upon the deck ready to run out quickly when the moment came. Already, three of the best line-throwers in the ship were crouched at the stern, ready to throw their heaving lines to the other ship, to which would be attached a grass rope, which would float downwind, bringing the tow rope on the end of it . . .

'Here she goes!' cried Brewster at Oakshott's elbow – as *Javelin*, halfway through her turn, rose on a mighty wavecrest, and paused. 'For what we are about to receive . . .'

The two men's hands almost met on the same hold. They stared into each other's face in the dawn light.

'If she doesn't roll right over on this one,' said Oakshott, 'she'll float for ever.'

The next huge comber caught *Javelin* in the trough of its predecessor, and beam on. It broke into white water well above the main topmast and bore her down in its irresistible weight and power. It is possible that her ribs came within an ace of cracking under the force: they sustained. The entire mast system could have been unseated when the ship heeled past the horizontal: it stood fast. Most of the men on deck could have been swept overboard; by a miracle, they clung on. Only one man was injured – and fatally – when one of the guns broke free of its lashing and went over the side, carrying a gallimaufry of torn flesh and shattered woodwork with it. *Javelin*'s fate hung in the balance for the longest few seconds that any man aboard her had experienced in his life – and then she righted herself and completed her turn towards the shore, her reefed sails taking the wind and driving her on.

The approach to the still anchored leader had vastly critical elements about it: if Oakshott calculated his turn too late, he might be borne down on to *Jaunty* in a fatal collision; too soon, and the vagaries of wind and water could carry the floundering *Javelin* too far clear of her consort. The ideal lay in turning the ship and stopping her within heaving-line distance – or close enough to float down the grass rope.

Meantime, she was running free on the following wind, raising her elegant stern obediently to every comber that came under her, and her sharp stem pointed directly at *Jaunty*.

'I like it this far,' said Oakshott grimly.

Five cables distance became four, and three in no time at all.

'I'll take the chance of closing with her as near as I dare,' said Oakshott, 'for we could both be on the putty before I have the chance to make another round. You may be sure that, with the kind of luck we've had tonight, the tide's on the ebb!

'Stand by to pass the tow, Number One.'

'Aye, aye, sir!'

'And – Thomas . . .

'Good luck!'

'Thank you, sir.' Brewster grinned.

Commodore Sir James Freakley, Bart, RN – Lucky Jimmy to all – was, in his own phrase, 'Broached to'.

The first of the savage combers that had struck *Jaunty* in the process of turning to come to anchor had caused the commodore to be thrown across his quarter-deck and halfway down the companionway. Cursing cheerfully, he had allowed himself to be carried to his stern cabin and bedded down. The ship's surgeon was summoned. Though himself chronically seasick, the latter needed only to lift his master's shirt and see the contusions upon the portly ribs, and note the trickle of bright blood that issued from the corner of the baronet's mouth, to know that Lucky Jimmy's fabled luck had at last seen fit to pass him by.

If Sir James repined that his overweight, over-indulged body was broken beyond mending, he did not show it, but called for a bumper of port wine, which he drank in fine style, and then demanded to be wrapped in oilskin and carried back up on deck. By this time it had been established that the damaged *Jaunty* – which he had prudently decided to anchor close inshore till the storm blew itself out – was dragging her cable, and he had given orders for Oakshott to take him in tow.

'Thank God it's young Oakshott,' growled the baronet. 'There's no captain in the navy in whom I repose more confidence than in Oakshott. I tell you truly.' And to his servant: 'Pour me another port, Wright, and mix it fifty-fifty with brandy. No short measures, mark you. When are those fellers coming to carry me back up top, damn their eyes?'

'Sir James,' said Wright, his right-hand man for twenty years, afloat and ashore, 'do you think it wise to be shifted? Best you remain here and I bring you swift news of all that passes aloft.'

'You are blethering again, Wright,' growled the commodore. 'Pass the word for those fellers to get down here sharply, or I'll have you flogged at the grating. And give me that glass. Don't fuss with me, man. I'm well capable of holding it myself. Oh, well, if you insist . . .'

In the event, when two stalwart seamen came to bear him up, the leader of the frigate squadron suffered a grave haemorrhage of his ruptured lung and was constrained to remain where he was, whilst the faithful Wright brought him constant and continuous information from the upper deck.

At first, it seemed to Oakshott that all was going well.

He turned *Javelin* as close to *Jaunty* as prudence dictated. The ship suffered the loss of some deck gear in the turning, no more. As she nicely drifted with her stern to the leader, the grass line was offered, and floated its way down as neatly as you please. The three hands with the heaving lines stood ready to display their expertise, each vying with the other for the commendations of their messmates that must follow for the first line across – not to mention the inevitable summons to the commodore when, in his best blues, the lucky sailor would receive a rummer of brandy from the leader's august hand, and a gold guinea for saving him, like as not.

And then – quite suddenly, in the way that disaster comes out of nowhere – everything began to go terribly wrong again . . .

Oakshott, who had had the thought to stream a sea anchor ahead of him to hold the ship to the wind, and had dismissed the notion as – in the swiftly-moving circumstances – an unnecessary elegance, soon had cause to repine. One monster wave, coming slightly askew of its companions, took *Javelin* fine on the port bow and began to turn her.

(No captain's judgement is all perfection all the time.)

So it was that, by the time *Javelin* came within heaving-line distance of her leader, she was already on the way to being broached to by the next big wave that took her. Moreover, the grass rope, instead of floating down to the leader, had taken on a sullen reluctance, had snarled itself in a tangle and was just lying there.

It all depended upon the three men with the heaving lines.

First Lieutenant Brewster was supervising the towing arrangements from the taffrail, where the three men were crouched.

'One at a time, lads!' he shouted above the howl of the storm. 'Take your time. Take it steady!'

The first to throw was Able Seaman Crouch, an East Anglian from Southwold. His line rose to a promising apogee, but the turk's head knot on its end fell into the water some ten feet away from the eager hands that reached out to grasp it.

'Next!' shouted Brewster.

Next was Able Seaman Buller, a Cornishman. He fared no better.

'It's all up to you, Mudge!' cried Brewster.

The giant Mudge – long-serving shipmate of Charles Oakshott, through three commissions and much hazard, ever since the latter had had him pressganged on his wedding morn – took stance to throw.

'God be with you, Mudge,' breathed Oakshott from the mizzen chains, 'for there's none like you.'

Mudge's throw did not take a high trajectory, but was more to be likened (and was, indeed, so likened by little Midshipman Cobbold, a promising Classics scholar before he took a passion to join the navy) to the flat and powerful deliveries of the discus throwers of Ancient Greece. Aimed straight at *Jaunty*'s bowsprit, the turk's head digressed neither to left nor right, up nor down, but sailed over the leader's heads and slammed against the base of her foremast. A cheer rang out from both *Jaunty* and *Javelin* as the line was taken and the tow gathered in.

This intelligence was brought down to the commodore, lying in his stern cabin.

'Sir James, the tow from *Javelin* has been taken aboard, sir,' said his faithful servant, bending low over the prostrate form that lay with eyes closed. And brought the response of a glad smile.

With *Javelin* made fast to her leader, Oakshott now had to battle with wind and tide – and the loss of his headsails – to shift his tow out to deep water. This proved to be an impossibility. No sooner had the stout hemp taken the strain when a call came over the water from *Jaunty*, who had just that moment raised her anchor.

'Sir, *Jaunty* says she's aground – hard. Stuck on the putty.' This from Cobbold.

'What to do, sir?' This from Brewster.

Oakshott drew a deep breath and much benefited from the same.

'Make all sail, Number One,' he said. 'We'll go out of this close-hauled, with *Jaunty* in tow. Or we'll stay on the putty, the pair of us.'

To give Oakshott his due, it was a bold decision, but the only alternative to doing nothing. The raising of full sail in such a gale of wind as this would, in normal circumstances, have been a folly beyond belief and likely to have brought disaster in its train; on the other hand, *Javelin*'s attachment to her leader gave, if nothing else, a certain steadying force . . .

The sails having been set: 'Lay her on the starboard tack!'

Her canvas straining to bursting, *Javelin* lay over sharply to port till the ends of her yardarms touched white water.

Down on the quarter-deck, Oakshott winced – to hear the main topgallant sail blow out into shreds like a cannon shot. And the mizzen royal immediately followed.

He met First Lieutenant Brewster's eye in the dawn light.

'She's not shifting, sir,' said the American.

Oakshott nodded.

'Maintain the present course, Number One,' he responded.

Then there came a cry from the masthead: 'Sail on the starboard bow – fine. A battleship. I don't see her colours, but she do look almighty like a Froggie sixty-four!'

'Action stations!' said Oakshott. 'Beat to quarters!'

Oakshott did not give the order to cast off the tow, but reduced sail so as to give himself the maximum amount of mobility if it came to a battle in the appalling circumstances.

In one and a half minutes (by Oakshott's watch), the crew was closed up for action.

'All guns load!'
'Search your piece!'
'Put home your powder!'
'Put home your wad!'
'Regard your shot!'
'Put home your shot!'
'Wad your shot!'
'Prick and prime your piece! . . .'

Within a minute, *Javelin*'s battery of thirty-two guns were run out and ready for action – though it has to be added that most of those on the port – leeward – side had already been sluiced by the white water that poured in from the open gun ports and would in all likelihood misfire to the last one.

The battleship came in sight to those on deck.

'She's a Frog all right, sir,' said Brewster, training his glass. 'They've a way of shaping the stem that's quite unmistakable.'

'Or Frog-built,' said Oakshott. 'Do you see her colours yet, Number One?'

'No, sir.'

It was the ever-watchful little Midshipman Cobbold who provided the intelligence for his seniors:

'She's flying the Danish ensign!'

'By God, he's right,' said Oakshott, sighting the white cross on red that streamed from the battleship's stern. 'Well, here's a fine kettle of fish – and we caught with our breeches down in our neighbour's back garden.'

The high-sided (obviously French-built) sixty-four made small beer of the appalling conditions and came about smartly three cables' length from the two British frigates. And stood there, aback.

A hail came over the water – in perfect English: *'Are you in trouble, gentlemen?'*

Oakshott exchanged glances with his first lieutenant.

'I fancy, Number One,' he said, 'that this is the moment

when we must address ourselves to eating a requisite amount of humble pie.'

'I guess you're right, sir,' opined the other.

Oakshott replied through a speaking trumpet: explaining his condition and that of his leader in some detail, contingent upon which the Dane closed and put across a tow line.

The battleship had no difficulty, with her spread of sail, in bringing both frigates safely off the lee shore together, and an hour or so later, in safe and deep water, and with the gale quite blown out – so that formations of geese were winging their ways over the three ships that wallowed in the calms at the approaches to the Skagerrak – Oakshott put on his full-dress coat and had himself and Pepe Lopez taken over to the Danish battleship, remarking on the way about the excellent seamanlike condition that the ship presented, with not a line of washing to be seen, nor a rope trailing over the side. Everything that should have been polished was polished, and everything that should have been thrust out of sight was thrust out of sight – Bristol fashion.

'Salute an English captain!'

The officer on the gangway spoke perfect English, so did the captain, who advanced to Oakshott and extended his hand.

'So pleased to have been of service to you – ah – Captain? . . .'

'Oakshott, sir,' responded the other, 'and this is my secretary, Señor Lopez. I am grateful for your timely and skilful assistance, for which I shall be – we shall all be – for ever indebted to you.'

The Dane, who introduced himself as Captain Larsen, was a man of about Oakshott's age and several inches taller. He carried himself with a quiet assurance and obviously possessed a considerable amount of the same quality in reserve.

'Thank you, Captain Oakshott,' said Larsen. 'Shall I have the pleasure of making the acquaintance of your colleague, the captain of the other frigate?'

'No, you will not, sir,' replied Oakshott. 'My leader, Commodore Sir James Freakley, died of injuries about the time you generously passed us your line, so I have been informed.'

They took wine in the commodious stern cabin. The Danish line-of-battle ship was named *Odense*. As Oakshott had guessed, she was French-built in Brest and purchased to order before the Revolution.

They proceeded with a formality that was perfectly acceptable to Oakshott, who was not given to slack manners. They toasted King George of England and King Christian of Denmark with great solemnity, and the fact that the former monarch was as mad as made no odds, and the latter a notorious degenerate, was not called to question.

That being done, a certain reserve closed down upon the company, which numbered five including Captain Larsen's first lieutenant and gunnery officer. All the Danes spoke excellent English.

After a short silence, Larsen regarded Oakshott quizzically.

'Captain, I think that your name is known to me,' he said, 'but I search my mind in vain for the connection.'

'The – um – affair of the *Hedeby*, perhaps?' suggested the other, who saw no point in mincing matters with so magnanimous a host.

'The *Hedeby* – ah!'

The three Danes looked at each other, then back at Oakshott.

'You acted strictly in accordance with your orders in that matter, sir,' said Larsen, straight-faced, thereby offering Oakshott the opportunity to get off the hook.

Oddly, the other did not feel constrained to succumb to the other's gentle ministration; instead, he pursued the point:

'Not so, sir,' he said. 'Indeed, I exceeded my brief in one regard, at least.'

'And what was that, sir?' asked the Dane.

'I put Captain Lehmann on his honour to enter Gibraltar and submit his charges to a search for contraband. That parole was not honoured.' Oakshott drained his glass upon delivering this statement, quite convinced that it would not be refilled.

The Danes were now in a swift and animated exchange in their own language. Oakshott glanced to Pepe Lopez, who gave him a nod of encouragement.

Presently the Danish captain turned to regard his guest again. 'Are you aware, Captain,' he said, 'that Lieutenant Lehmann – who is well known to me, having once served as midshipman under my command – has strenuously denied that he gave you any assurances of parole?'

'I am not one bit surprised to hear that, sir,' responded Oakshott.

The other's eyes narrowed. 'Do you imply, sir, that this officer – this fine young officer – is lying?'

'I do not,' responded Oakshott. 'From what I have heard, I *infer* that Lieutenant Lehmann did not receive the terms of the parole, which were addressed by me, in English, to the gentleman known as Count Axel Bernstorff.'

'Bernstorff – aaah!'

'Bernstorff!'

The Danes repeated the same to each other and looked wise. A noticeable relaxation of hostility permeated the atmosphere in the battleship's stern cabin. Larsen replenished all their glasses.

'You should know, Captain Oakshott,' said he, 'that Count Bernstorff stands very high in the councils of Europe. He sups with everyone' – here the other's shrewd eyes seemed to be trying to communicate more than mere words to his guest – 'and to serve the ends of his masters, whoever *they* are, would sup with the devil.'

'Then it's to be hoped,' said Oakshott, 'that the devil counts his spoons before and after supper.'

They all laughed.

'More seriously,' resumed Larsen, 'you should not take it that Bernstorff's actions aboard the *Hedeby* were necessarily directed to the advantage of Denmark – not in the long run, at least. So much one has learned about this person, who is known among the informed as The Mystery Man of Europe.'

'I look forward to meeting him again,' said Oakshott.

'From the way you said that, sir,' smiled Larsen, 'I would think it much to the count's advantage to give you a wide berth.'

Felicitations over, Larsen saw them over the side to their waiting boat. He and Oakshott shook hands.

'Again, thank you, sir,' said the latter. 'It is an irony that you should have saved two British ships, and their crews, when our two countries seem to be steering a collision course towards open hostilities.'

'I pray that it will never come to it, sir,' responded Larsen, retaining his grip on Oakshott's hand and pressing it firmly. 'The British and the Danes are cousins, and should never quarrel.'

The silvery pipes shrilled out. Oakshott doffed his hat in salute and followed Pepe Lopez down into the boat. He looked back at the high-sided ship-of-the-line as the oarsmen gave way together. The *Odense* was already shaking out her sails and turning in the slight swell to head off into the Skagerrak.

'Well, what did you make of all that, Pepe?' he asked his companion. 'Every time one turns over a flat stone, there's that fellow Bernstorff lurking underneath.'

'I'm thinking, sir,' said the other, 'that this Bernstorff – this Mystery Man of Europe as they dub him – who appears to be as *persona grata* in Whitehall as he is in a Danish ship entering Toulon with contraband – may not only have nearly brought you to a court martial, but also have saved you from it.'

Oakshott met the other's berry-black eyes and frowned.

'What *are* you implying, Pepe?' he demanded.

'Only that – in Chief Secretary Manthorpe's pencilled footnote to Their Lordships' dispatch – you have powerful friends in most unexpectedly high places. What did you – what *do* you – infer from that observation, sir?'

'Well,' said Oakshott, 'the only person in high places that would be likely to raise a finger to help me would be Lord Nelson, who has shown me some favours in the past.

'I suppose – I *suppose* I saw Nelson's hand there, in saving me from the court martial.

'As for Bernstorff! Oh, Pepe, you're being too over-subtle, as is often your wont.'

The other smiled his shrewd smile. 'Lord Nelson's hand you may dismiss in this instance, sir,' he said. 'For his lordship has been – as any subscriber to *The Times* newspaper knows – deeply engaged in the tangled politics of the Kingdom of the Two Sicilies since the victory of the Nile. Not to mention certain scandalous rumours we hear concerning his association with a certain lady who shall be nameless.

'No, sir, I do not see the hand of your mentor Lord Nelson here. His lordship has been far too busy in Naples and elsewhere to acquaint himself with the misfortunes of – with the greatest respect to you, sir – an obscure frigate captain back in England.

'No, sir. If I were a gambling man – which I am not – I would stake my money on Count Axel Bernstorff.'

'And I think you would lose your shirt, Pepe,' responded Oakshott.

He looked towards *Javelin* and *Jaunty*, both gently nodding together in the shallow troughs, both with their ensigns at mourning half mast.

'Well, as senior officer present and acting commodore,' he said, 'I must address myself to giving poor Sir James a sailor's funeral, and make sail back to Harwich, seeking out Captain Bolton and the *Arrow* along the way.

'I think one may take it that the powerful presence of our so-far friendly *Odense* has checkmated us in this particular game, Pepe. We may as well remove ourselves from the board.'

FIVE

July of that year found *Javelin* still in Harwich, but under orders to shift to the command of Admiral Dixon. Following the undoubted fiasco of Lucky Jimmy's last gamble, added to a continuing confusion in the policy of resisting the Armed Neutrality, the situation between Britain and the Baltic states was – literally – all at sea. To add fuel to the ill will, a Danish frigate named *Frija* had been captured in the Channel after a gun action, and brought to port along with her six merchantmen in convoy. The incident caused all diplomatic hell to be let loose, and Whitehall's response was to send a top diplomat to Copenhagen to sort out the mess. And Admiral Dixon's squadron was to sail into Copenhagen Sound – in order to make it clear to the Danes that diplomacy was not the only shot in Britain's locker.

Javelin received her orders to sail and join Dixon on the 18th of that month – a Friday.

'Ready in all respects to proceed to sea, sir.'

This was First Lieutenant Brewster's formal announcement to his captain as he stood before him in the latter's cabin, beplumed hat tucked under one arm, one elegant leg thrust forward like a dancing master's, one hand on sword-dressed hip.

Oakshott presciently detected the slight hesitation in the other's voice. 'Only – *what*, Number One?' he quizzed.

'Only – Able Seaman Mudge went adrift last night, sir.'

'Not Mudge!' cried Oakshott, rising to his feet in dismay and pushing aside the remains of his breakfast. 'Surely not. Not *Mudge!*'

'Was apprehended by a shore patrol whilst attempting to board a coach to London, sir,' said the other. 'Moreover, he put up a tough fight. One, at least, of the shore patrol will carry the marks to his grave.'

'Oh, God, this is awful – *awful!*' said Oakshott.

Mudge! The man he had pressganged on his wedding day. The stalwart of three commissions. The giant who had lent his brute strength and cool courage in a score of tight corners. Whose son, moreover, was named after Oakshott and was his godchild.

Oakshott met Brewster's eye: they both know the score. Desertion – or attempted desertion – was a summary hanging matter in wartime, and only protracted in peacetime by the processes of a court martial.

'Where is he now?' asked Oakshott.

'Back aboard,' replied Brewster. 'Up in the forepeak under guard. The officer in command of the shore party – one Lieutenant Newman – refuses to relinquish control over his prisoner and his own men are guarding Mudge. I rather fancy, sir – it seems to me – that the bloodthirsty bastard is expecting you to order Mudge to be hanged from the mizzen peak before we depart on the tide in an hour's time.'

'Have Mudge brought to me, Number One,' breathed Oakshott.

'Aye, aye, sir!'

'And keep the egregious Mr Newman out of here. And his men.'

'Yes, *sir!*' Brewster looked relieved.

They brought him in, the prisoner. Two of his own messmates now guarded him, cutlasses on hip. But there was no need of them. Mudge looked like a stunned ox, his great head bowed on his chest, revealing a livid bruise along the hairline, where a cudgel had taken him. There was blood – his or another's – on his shirt front. And his wrists were roped.

'Unbind him!' ordered Oakshott. And this was done.

'Now, tell me, Mudge,' said his captain. 'What's all this about, hey? Speak up, man.'

The giant raised his head and fixed Oakshott with his mild blue eyes that held an appeal, but something else – a touch of defiance? wondered *Javelin*'s captain.

'It wuz how I *had* to go, sir,' said Mudge. 'Back home to Dartmouth, like.'

'Why, man?'

No reply.

'Mudge, you must tell me the reason,' said Oakshott. 'There is an officer out there who will wish me to stick by the letter of the law and hang you before the tide. If there's anything you can say in your defence, you'd better out with it, or your wife will be a widow by noon, and my godson fatherless.'

In respect to that, Mudge muttered something only half-audible, which, Oakshott having taken in and reassembled it, added up to something very odd.

'Did I hear aright?' asked Oakshott, astounded. 'Or did you say something to the effect that your wife would rejoice to hear it?'

'I don't say she,' responded the other with some truculence, 'but there's some in Dartmouth who might think 'tis safer for them if she be widowed.'

Oakshott drew a deep breath and exhaled it slowly through his nostrils.

'Mudge, you will admit that I have been very patient with you,' he said, 'but the time has come when you must stop talking in riddles. Why did you go adrift last night and attempt to take post to London, and then on – I suppose –

to your home town of Dartmouth? Answer me short, man.'

Mudge nodded. 'Sir, I did have this letter,' he said.

'A letter – ah! From your wife?'

'No, sir. It wuz read aloud to me by Able Seaman Teal, who is a scholar. But it wuz not from my wife, nor did anybody take down her words, like.'

'Do you have this letter with you?'

For answer, Mudge groped in the pocket of his white sailcloth pantaloons and brought forth a folded piece of paper which he passed over to his captain. Oakshott took it. Much folded and refolded, bearing the marks of many tarry fingerprints and obviously greatly pored-over, every word painfully mouthed over and over again by unschooled scholars on the messdeck, it bore a short message written in a crabbed and curiously ugly hand that epitomized the dripping evil which had fallen from the pen.

To Tom Mudge

It were a fine thing for the wife of a brave tar to be giving herself airs and graices in silks and geegaws wile her man be giving his blude for king and countree be known tom mudge that your shaymeless wife be turned STRUMPET while you have gone and does CONSORT with the GENTLEMEN of the town the likes of the SQUIRE the PARSON the DOCTOR and others and the squire when he was taken to task that you would like to kill him when you came hoame did say let that mudge set foot at my door and ill have him hoarsewipped away

A Well Wisher

Poor devil, thought Oakshott. Poor gullible devil. And a 'Well Wisher' of fiendishly subtle sort. The cleverest part of the vile missive, the sting in the tail that would drive any jealous cuckold to fury, was the goad that he would be thwarted out of any attempt at revenge by a whipping at the hands of the squire's hobbledehoys. That was a touch well worthy of Shakespeare's Iago.

How did that gentleman so subtly express his philosophy? . . .

> Trifles light as air
> Are to the jealous confirmations strong
> As proofs of holy writ.

Oakshott held out the letter to the scowling giant.

'Tell me, Mudge,' he said. 'Do you – *did* you – truly believe what is written here of your wife?'

The other shuffled his feet and dropped his gaze.

'I – I had no ways of a-telling, sir,' he mumbled. 'Save to go along and find out for meself.'

'And in so doing put yourself in hazard of the noose!' snapped Oakshott. 'Why did you not make a request to come and see me, show me the letter, and determine what could be done to help you?

'Mudge – Mudge, you are a valued man and a staunch shipmate. The navy will go that extra mile, and a mile again, to help its own. You should know that!'

Something like a tear began in the corner of the giant's mild, washed-out blue eyes.

'I be sorry, sir,' he whispered. 'That I should ha' done. I know it now, right enough.'

'It's still not too late,' said Oakshott. 'Mr Secretary!'

'Sir!' Pepe Lopez, standing discreetly behind and to one side of his master, took two smart paces forward.

'Dispatch with all speed a memorandum to the Naval Officer in Charge, Dartmouth. Give my respects to the NOIC and call his attention to a copy of this letter, lately received by a seaman in this ship. Beg him to make discreet inquiries as to the wellbeing of the lady (you will apprise Captain Hawker of Mrs Mudge's address) and advise me at his earliest convenience. Is that clear?'

'Perfectly clear, sir. I will have the memorandum dispatched before we leave.' Pepe bobbed his nearest equivalent to a salute and scurried away.

Oakshott turned to regard Mudge again.

'I've not the slightest doubt, Mudge, that your admirable lady wife will be most puzzled – but also flattered – to have a courtesy visit from one of Captain Hawker's officers inquiring as to her health,' he said. 'Furthermore, if she has any complaint of molestation by whoever it was who wrote the letter, I think we can rely upon the NOIC to handle that, also.

'And now – get about your duties!'

Mudge's jaw fell. 'Cap'n, sir – do you mean? . . .' he faltered.

'Your years of good service have saved your neck this time, Mudge,' said Oakshott. 'But will not like to do so a second time.

'Get you gone!'

The giant needed no further bidding.

Oakshott met Brewster's eye.

'And what shall I tell Lieutenant Newman, sir?' asked the latter.

Oakshott reflected for a moment.

'Tell him, Number One, that justice has been done,' he said.

'Ah – with respect, sir,' rejoined the other, 'what if the gentleman in question prefers to *see* justice being done according to his lights?'

'Then he will be disappointed, Number One.'

Brewster persisted. 'But what if he lays a complaint – and I tell you sir, that he looks a most complainingful young man – before his superior that justice has not been seen to be done? I pose the question as a hypothesis, merely.'

'Well then, Number One,' said Oakshott, 'to that I will counter the hypothesis that, before we return to Harwich, a ball may have taken off Mudge's head, in which case justice will have been seen to have been done – and incidentally saved the navy the price of three fathoms of hemp rope and a noose.'

And with a grin, the captain of *Javelin* tucked his telescope under his arm and went up on deck to view the preparations for leaving harbour.

The American watched him go, and shook his head. There is a man, thought Brewster, who would hazard his cherished career for a humble Jack Tar. Small wonder they'd all follow him anywhere.

And so would I – God help me!

After a good solo passage *Javelin* sailed by way of the Skagerrak and Kattegat to the complex of islands that make up Denmark and the entrances to the Baltic. Possessing only the most rudimentary charts – some of them hand drawn – the frigate presently closed with Copenhagen Sound, which is a channel some four miles wide at its narrowest part, with Sweden to port and the island of Zeeland to starboard. It was here, closing with the narrows, that a cutter bearing the White Ensign approached the newcomer and hailed that she was putting a pilot aboard to take them on into Copenhagen Roads.

The pilot was a Dutchman named Drees. Oakshott, whose introduction to the present war with France had been an action in the company of a Dutch merchant skipper,* held Hollanders in high regard and was grateful for Drees's assistance.

They sailed in good deep water through the narrows, with the pilot pointing to features of interest. Oakshott's keenly tactical mind quickly assembled very clear views about the defences of the Danish capital.

'There, sir,' said Drees, pointing, 'is Kronborg Castle and the citadel of Elsinore.'

*See the first Oakshott novel, *Run Out the Guns* (Century 1984)

'Elsinore!' said Oakshott, aiming his telescope. 'Shades of Prince Hamlet! I would not care to pass this way under fire from those frowning ramparts!' He swept his glass to port, to the Swedish shore. 'Nor if the Swedes took a notion to bar one's passage, also, that fortification opposite would make it a running of the gauntlet one would not soon forget.'

'True, sir,' responded the Dutchman. 'You are looking at the fortress of Helsingborg. As you say, Captain, forcing the approaches to Copenhagen could be most unpleasant – particularly if the Swedes joined in.' His keen, reflective glance had already taken the measure of the Englishman, and approved of what he saw.

Past a small island in the widening part of the sound, they presently came in sight of a forest of masts and a galaxy of towers, domes and steeples that marked the Danish seaport and capital. Towards noon of that day, with the tide on the ebb, the most informative Drees brought them to an anchorage on the edge of a mixed fleet of warships and merchantmen in about six fathoms, some two miles from a most potent-looking, star-shaped fortress that dominated the right-hand entrance to the city's harbour.

'That, sir, is the Citadel,' said Drees. 'And there' – pointing to a pair of forts built on piles and dominating the approach on the opposite side – 'there are the Trekroner batteries. So, you see, even in nominal time of peace, Copenhagen is – formidable.'

Oakshott saw it all too clearly.

Oakshott was taking his midday meal alone in the stern cabin with a copy of the ship's accounts propped up against the salt cellar when a visitor was announced.

'Walker, sir – Flag Lieutenant to Admiral Dixon, at your service. So sorry to disturb you, but . . .'

'Take a seat, Mr Walker,' said Oakshott, shaking the other's hand. 'I've just finished. Some wine?'

'Thank you, sir.' Walker was the epitome of the flag lieutenant, being young, good-looking, ingratiating, impeccably turned out and devastatingly self-confident. Oakshott had the wayward wish that the cabin was cleaner and fresh napery provided at the table – but instantly dismissed the thought.

'Your very good health, Mr Walker,' said he. 'So – do you bring me news from the flagship?'

'Your health also, Lord Charles,' said the other. 'As to news, there is none save that our emissary Lord Whitworth is striving to make some settlement with the Danes whereby, in return for our restoring the frigate *Frija* and her convoy of merchantmen, he hopes to persuade the Danes to abandon the convoy system. However, the fly in the ointment – if I may be permitted the phrase – is Tsar Paul who, though nominally at war with the French, is definitely trailing his cloak in Boney's direction and may seize upon the *Frija* incident to change sides and drag the Baltic states in along with him.'

Oakshott nodded. 'Are there any French sail in or near the Baltic?' he asked, recalling poor Lucky Jimmy's fond hope of engaging and defeating an enemy sixty-four with his tiny squadron.

'We have no knowledge of any, sir,' replied Walker, 'though they have undoubtedly penetrated into the Baltic – and one may be sure that the Danes, at least, will be looking the other way when they pass through. At least, that's my view.'

'Most interesting,' was Oakshott's comment to that. 'More wine, Mr Walker?'

'Thank you, sir,' said the hugely self-confident flag lieutenant. 'Which brings me to my primary reason for calling upon you today – apart from welcoming you to the squadron on behalf of the admiral' – here he paused and smilingly accepted Oakshott's graceful inclination of the head – 'which is to inform you that your presence will be required at a reception to be held in the Christiansborg palace this evening. It will be a highly formal occasion at which our ships' captains may, or may not, be presented to the king. In any event, Lord Whitworth is most anxious to make a good showing. Starting at eight bells from the flagship, a cutter will call upon every ship of the squadron and pick up the captain and one other officer - *not* the second in command. The admiral wishes to impress upon the squadron that we are here in Copenhagen on a quasi-war footing and that all ships must remain at two minutes' notice for action.'

'With or without me, *Javelin*'s time for coming into action is one minute and a half, Mr Walker,' murmured Oakshott. 'More wine?'

To cover any contingency of language, Oakshott had ordered Pepe Lopez to accompany him to the reception. Accordingly, as eight bells of the last dog watch rang out, the captain's secretary was waiting by the gangway in his best silk coat of clerical grey with breeches to match, and a cloak over his arm.

The cutter arrived soon after and Oakshott followed his companion down into the boat, where amongst the officers seated there were several familiar faces: frigate captains including Sam Sutton of *Alcmene* and Edward Riou of *Amazon*. Also Bolton of *Arrow*, Oakshott's fellow consort on Lucky Jimmy's last venture.

There was a space on the thwart beside Riou, and Oakshott took it. One of the finest and best-liked of the navy's senior frigate captains, Riou was a man of splendid bearing, handsome of countenance, who affected side whiskers with the hair *en brosse*, after the new mode. The two captains exchanged reminiscences of past encounters and speculations about the present situation with Denmark and the Baltic states. They continued their discourse till the cutter was within a short distance of the menacing Trekroner batteries, when Riou broke off to direct the helmsman to shape course as close to the forts as possible – and prudently.

'We'll see what the Danes have got up there on those forts, Oakshott,' he declared.

It became clear that the twin forts were built upon piles, a ship's length distant from each other, on the very edge of the shallows commanding the port-hand side of the harbour entrance, with the ability to fire upon the anchorage where Dixon's squadron and others were lying. As the boatload of officers drew close, a line of unsmiling faces peered down on them from the high ramparts of the nearest fort, through whose machicolations could be seen the menacing dark muzzles of heavy cannon.

'Mixed twenty-four and thirty-six-pounders,' said Oakshott. 'And there must be over thirty up there.'

'I count thirty-four,' said Riou. 'By heaven, Oakshott, any force approaching from the anchorage would have to contend with the equivalent of two battleships' broadsides.'

'It would take a hard morning's work to pound 'em to silence.'

'It would indeed, Oakshott,' grinned the other. 'But a worthy enterprise.'

They said no more upon the subject, but the incident – and Edward Riou's remark – would return most forcibly to Oakshott's mind in the not so distant future . . .

A small fleet of closed carriages was awaiting them at the quayside when they alighted, and they were directed to be seated, four to a carriage. They were then driven through the streets in procession; past ancient, gabled houses of very fine appearance, through imposing open squares where marble statuary gestured flamboyantly, over innumerable bridges. If the crowds in the streets paid any interest to the column of coaches, each bearing four grim-faced men in high-cocked hats, they did not show it.

It was dusk when the convoy reached the royal palace and drew rein at the foot of a sweeping flight of steps ascending to massive portals. A scarlet carpet had been laid up the entire length of the steps, and the balustrades were lined at each side by liveried menservants in brass-bound coats and powdered wigs, bearing flambeaux that gave a dramatically rosy hue to the scene.

Oakshott and his companions joined the throng of fellow guests mounting up to the double doors of the palace, where their names were taken by a major-domo who passed on each separate guest, along with his name, to another functionary who, when the person concerned had been relieved of his hat and cloak, then announced the new arrival in a voice that would have shamed any town crier back in England.

And, presently . . .

'CAPTAIN LORD CHARLES OAKSHOTT, ROYAL NAVY!'

Followed by . . .

'SEÑOR LOPEZ!'

Oakshott and Pepe Lopez strolled in through a mass of glittering uniforms and decorations, powdered wigs, the glint of women's brilliant costumes, heady scent of expensive perfumes; and it seemed to the captain of *Javelin* that they, and every Britisher announced, was treated to the most searching looks from all present; from the assembled Danes, there was not so much as a raised eyebrow to betray animosity. It was simply that – *they stared* . . .

The reception chamber was of massive proportions and its painted ceiling bore representations of innumerable swirling figures of heroic size. A dozen huge chandeliers lit the scene with countless pinpoints of candle flame augmented a thousandfold from the faceted crystal pendants. At the far end of the chamber was laid an enormous buffet table set – as Oakshott was swift to notice – with cold comestibles of the most soignée kind, mostly composed of fish of every conceivable species, and presented with an abundance of sauces and garnishes in prodigious variety.

A waiter brought Oakshott and his secretary a salver bearing champagne; each took a glass and eyed the other over the raised rim.

'This puts me in mind of a similar function I attended in Naples,' said Oakshott. 'But only because of the remarkable disparity between the two occasions. At Lady Hamilton's reception almost everyone was well advanced into either fornication or gluttony or both. And everyone was drunk. On the other hand, this has the indefinable overtones of a well-attended wake. I don't see a smile anywhere.'

'Nor are they partaking of that magnificent buffet in any number, sir,' responded his secretary. 'Might I suggest that this would be an opportune time for you and me to help ourselves?' Pepe Lopez, a man of most civilized manners, had spent many years of his life in slavery after having been sold in the marketplace of Algiers, and he still retained the slave's prudent way of eating as much as possible whenever it was on offer, lest he should want on the morrow.

Together they moved over to the buffet where, before a mountainous confection of shellfish set in a bed of ice crystals, they were joined by Bolton of *Arrow*. The latter had contrived to corner for himself a market in champagne: he had a serving lad following him around with a laden salver.

'Oakshott, I've been talking to one of our army people on Lord Whitworth's staff,' he said. 'He tells me that the talks are going badly.'

'How badly?' asked the other.

Bolton shrugged. 'The Danes won't give way an inch and are almost certainly in continuous communication with the Tsar and possibly taking counsel from him.' He chuckled. 'Eat up, my dear fellow, while the going's good. We might well have to fight our way back to the ships.' Bolton had a well-developed sense of dark humour.

Having made fair inroads into the buffet, the two from *Javelin* took champagne glasses in hand and strolled round the thronged chamber, exchanging nods with familiar faces and receiving blank stares from the Danes. They had done one complete turn of the floor when Pepe laid a hand on his captain's arm as if to make a casual remark. Oakshott paused to listen. The remark was far from casual – and inflected with the Hispano-Moor's sense of drama and intrigue: 'Sir, do not turn to look about you. There is a lady – a most beautiful lady – who has not taken her eyes off you since we began our *paseo*.'

'Interesting!' replied Oakshott, obediently keeping his eyes to the front. 'Whereabouts is she, Pepe? And tell me when I may prudently look in her direction.'

'She is seated against the wall, immediately behind you, under a large picture of a seascape. There are two officers with her – they are in Danish naval uniform. She has no eyes or ears for them. Only for you, sir.'

'Then I must take the chance of causing her embarrassment by outfacing her,' said Oakshott, turning.

And then he was back in Mogg's Diversions on a cold winter's night, with the threat of a court-martial hanging like the sword of Damocles over his head, and a stranger was watching him through the heat and the tobacco smoke of the crowded room.

No longer wearing a Venetian mask, she revealed herself to possess the nature and quality of beauty that he had imagined back in Mogg's, but imperfectly, for – as on the previous occasion – she had a quizzing glass held to her eyes.

It was she. There was not the slightest doubt in Oakshott's mind.

Looking straight at him, as she had done before. And smiling.

It was then – just as Oakshott was about to move towards

his Unknown – that an orchestra, which had newly taken its place in a minstrel gallery above the buffet table, struck up a martial-sounding air.

'Stand still and to attention, old fellow,' came a voice at his shoulder – it was Bolton's. 'This is the Danish national anthem, and, if I'm not mistaken, here comes King Christian the Seventh himself, God have mercy on the poor, benighted wretch!'

The royal entourage entered the reception chamber through an ornate archway and down a flight of steps lined with guardsmen in helmets and cuirasses, sabres drawn. First came a pair of richly-tabarded gentlemen bearing wands of office. Reaching the foot of the stair they parted, each to one side, and bowed deeply. Next came two elderly officers – generals or marshals, both – carrying drawn swords before them. After these gentlemen-at-arms followed a male person who could have been any age between fifty and eighty: hunched, shambling, suspicious eyes flickering from side to side, idiot mouth agape. He wore a simple coat of midnight blue, adorned on the left breast with the star of an order. This creature, as Oakshott immediately discerned, was His Majesty King Christian VII of Denmark.

As the king took his place on a scarlet carpet near the foot of the stair with his courtiers, guards and retainers formed behind him, the gentlemen in the tabards beckoned to the assembled company to form into line to be presented to the monarch. Oakshott took his place with the rest, and found Bolton of *Arrow* at his back.

'Regard him, the poor bastard,' murmured Bolton in Oakshott's ear. 'Regard – and search your philosophy for reasons why the Fates should bestow unimaginable splendour with one hand and sprinkle utter degradation with the other.

'Consider him – king at seventeen. Married to the sister of our present most illustrious monarch. But by this time he had been thoroughly debauched in Greek practices and his mind was turned, and he became entirely under the thumb of his chief minister Struensee . . .'

Bolton was drunk, but perfectly articulate. Oakshott, who knew most – but not all – of the sketch of the Danish monarch's life and career, fervently hoped that his comrade in arms' well-honed asides were not being overheard.

'However, the despicable Struensee came to a bad end. He was executed for adultery with the queen – a scandal which must have caused our present illustrious monarch some embarrassment. One hears, however, that the Crown Prince Frederick is now really king in all but name, which adds a touch of pathos to this present farcical charade.

'Oh dear – what's happening now?'

A fair number of the guests had been presented to the king by the wand-bearers. This required the person concerned to step forward, bow, or curtsy to the curious figure in the simple coat of midnight blue – a gesture which was returned by a blank stare – and then retire backwards. This process having been repeated without variation for a while, the king grew suddenly petulant: muttering to himself, looking from side to side, shuffling his slippered feet and waving his arms. Finally, without so much as a by your leave, he pushed his way through the ranks of his courtiers and scurried on up the stairs and out of sight. The appalled silence which followed the sovereign's departure was broken by a far-off, manic peal of laughter from somewhere above that echoed and re-echoed across the vast painted ceiling of the reception chamber.

'Well,' murmured Bolton. 'It's to be hoped that never again will that poor, benighted wretch be dragged out to put a gloss upon an occasion.'

'Excuse me a moment, Bolton,' said Oakshott.

The line of guests awaiting presentation being in the act of breaking up, Oakshott seized his opportunity to resume the enterprise upon which he had been about to launch himself when the National Anthem had struck up. Elbowing his way through the throng and peering over powdered heads, he searched for a sign of his Unknown. With a sudden sense of irremediable loss, he saw that the sofa upon which she had been sitting was now occupied by two chattering matrons. Of the officers who had been in the Unknown's company there was no sign either.

Bereft, he stared about him, searching the throng for the enigma with the quizzing glass.

A hand touched his elbow – gently and with great deference.

Oakshott spun round, hope in his heart – to face a liveried lackey, who had to raise his voice considerably to make himself heard above the parakeet chatter all round them.

'Lord Charles – an old acquaintance bids the pleasure of your company *à deux*. Will you please follow me, my lord?'

His guide took him out of the reception chamber by way of double doors leading to a long corridor hung on one side with portraits of long-gone monarchs, princes and high dignitaries set in heavy gilt frames. On the other, a succession of tall, unshuttered windows looked out across the city lights and the summer night sky splattered with stars.

A staircase followed, and yet another corridor, at the end of which the lackey paused by a gilded door and knocked. A low voice answered from within.

The man opened the door and, standing aside to allow Oakshott to enter, announced his presence.

The door closed behind Oakshott. He found himself in a long room with wide windows at the far end that looked out on to a terrace and a lantern-hung garden set with statuary of the classical sort. Save for the loom of light coming in from the garden, there was no other form of illumination in the room; but Oakshott saw a movement and discerned that someone was seated close by the window, the head part-silhouetted.

'Good evening,' murmured the captain of *Javelin* as he advanced to meet this – 'old acquaintance'.

And then a hand was suddenly revealed as it reached and removed a shade from a candlestick. The light of the single candle played on a pale and well-formed face, and one iridescent blue eye that was turned upon the Englishman; the other was hidden by a patch.

'Good evening, Captain Oakshott,' responded Count Axel Bernstorff.

SIX

If Oakshott's hand instinctively moved towards the hilt of the dress sword at his hip, it was only by a fraction. Instantly recovering his composure, he addressed the other, who was engaged upon lighting a three-branch candelabrum – whilst never taking his single eye from Oakshott for an instant.

'Well met, Count!' said the latter. 'A pity this is not England – in which case I would have had the pleasure of asking my seconds to call upon you.'

Bernstorff smiled. 'So direct!' he murmured. 'The typical man of action. And what pleasure would you have derived, my friend, from shooting the head off a one-eyed man?'

'I would have rid my country, and all Europe, of one I have learned, through informed sources and from personal experience, to be a thoroughgoing, two-faced scoundrel!' responded Oakshott.

Nor did this declaration cause the smile to falter upon that bland countenance. Instead, still smiling, Bernstorff walked over to a console table where stood a carafe of wine, and filled two glasses.

'When we have finished our discourse, Oakshott,' he said, 'and when you have heard my tale, we shall part from here as the best of friends. In anticipation of this, will you not take wine with me?'

He advanced one of the glasses and Oakshott took it – but stiff-faced.

'Here's to – *victory*,' said the one-eyed man.

'By all means I'll drink to that,' responded Oakshott. 'But whose victory do you have in mind?'

'Ours – yours and mine,' was the enigmatic response.

'That could pose certain complications,' said Oakshott. 'A case of pull devil, pull baker, perhaps?'

'Our interests are not in opposition, Oakshott,' replied the other.

'Indeed?' Oakshott cocked a doubtful eye at his companion. 'Touching upon our late encounter aboard the *Hedeby* and what followed, I would say that our interests have been demonstrably in opposition!'

'Ah, it was about that I wanted to talk to you, Oakshott,' said Bernstorff. 'Will you not sit down, drink your wine, and hear me out?'

Oakshott shrugged and took his place in a wing chair close by the window, facing his companion.

'Pray proceed, Count,' he said. 'You have the floor.'

'But feel free to interpose if there is anything I do not make clear,' said Bernstorff, 'or if I make any statement with which you are in disagreement.'

'Be sure that I will.'

'Very well, then.' Bernstorff relaxed in his seat, crossed one elegantly clad leg over his knee, flicked an imaginary speck of dust from the discreet frill of lace at his shirt cuff, and began: 'I am assuming you are now aware that the *Hedeby*'s convoy was not only carrying contraband when we encountered you, but also that more war *matériel* was taken aboard in North Africa and landed in Toulon. Correct?'

Oakshott inclined his head.

'So much for the external facts,' said Bernstorff. 'Now to the internal truths. You may not have appreciated, Oakshott – and certainly have not been informed – that the entire operation, of supplying the port and garrison of Toulon with war *matériel*, was conceived and carried out by me on behalf of the Danish government, not, I hasten to add, for any base commercial advantage, but for the political purpose of ingratiating Denmark with Bonaparte – to Denmark's eventual advantage. Do you follow?'

'I follow perfectly,' said Oakshott. 'But how does that alter the case? You were treating with England's enemy – hence, you were breaking the code of neutrality – in our eyes.'

Bernstorff did not reply till he had taken a long sip of his wine. When he had done so he replaced the glass upon the side table and smiled across at his companion, his half-profile dramatically lit by the candles.

'I now have to tell you that the internal workings of the conspiracy – for conspiracy it was in every sense – came very close to ruination when you sought to impose a parole upon *Hedeby*'s captain to enter Gibraltar and be discovered.

'*Our masters were not pleased by your action, Oakshott!*'

'You mean *your* masters were not pleased, Bernstorff!' was the other's vehement reponse. 'And to hell with them!'

A pause . . .

And then Bernstorff leaned forward, and in a very gentle voice said: 'When I say *our* masters I mean precisely that, Oakshott.'

He paused . . .

'Upon my return from Toulon, I journeyed to London, secured an interview with Prime Minister Pitt, and persuaded him that not only Denmark, but also Britain would stand to gain from my having Bonaparte's ear with my convoy of contraband. And he fully agreed.

'However, some fool of a lieutenant submitted a report about your action, and your goose was cooked – as they say.'

Oakshott, shocked to silence, could only listen and speculate.

'Your devotion to duty came close to ruining my conspiracy, Oakshott,' said Bernstorff. 'If the captain of the *Hedeby* had understood English he would have accepted the parole and acted upon it. For he is a stiff-necked officer and a dyed-in-the-wool Danish gentleman, of that I assure you.

'You really did deserve that court martial, Oakshott. You cannot conceive what a success, in the event, my stratagem has been. When I tell you that Bonaparte has invited me to attend him at Versailles at my convenience! Think of it! . . .

'*I have become the eyes and ears of all Europe!*'

Oakshott watched, fascinated, as the other rose to his feet and began pacing up and down in the gloom of the candlelight, gesticulating in a frenzy of self-adulation.

'Now Pitt consults me about everything concerning Denmark, and will shortly do likewise concerning France. Later, I shall extend my influence to the Court of St Petersburg.' He paused and pointed an accusatory finger at Oakshott. 'Lord Charles, I have to tell you that Pitt was determined on your court martial and disgrace for that blundering act of overzealousness which – but for my keeping the terms of your parole from young Lieutenant Lehmann – could have ruined everything!'

Oakshott passed his hand across his brow. Maybe he had drunk too much champagne, but his mind could not come to terms with the web of intrigue and mad paradox that was being unwound before him.

He had to reach hold of reality and pin it down . . .

'A moment, Bernstorff, if you please . . .' he pleaded.

'By all means, Oakshott.'

'In my simplicity,' said the other, 'I was of the impression that Mr Pitt was going to have me court martialled for dereliction of duty . . .'

'A lesser man would have done just that,' replied Bernstorff. 'But Pitt, in his sublime vision, realized the larger implications of your action. His first reaction was to crush you like an ant for having so nearly foiled my masterly plan.'

'Was it, by God,' growled Oakshott. 'Then damn him – and damn you, too!'

'However,' continued the bland Bernstorff, 'the Prime Minister's inherent good nature quickly supervened. It took little to persuade him to wash out the court-martial proceedings.'

Oakshott stared at his companion. From somewhere out of the dark recesses of his undoubtedly drink-befuddled mind there emerged the glimmerings of a great truth.

He pointed at his companion.

'You, Bernstorff!' he cried. 'It *was* you – you the so-called "friend in high places" who got me off the hook!

'But why, man – *why?*'

The other came towards him, carafe in hand, and recharged the Englishman's glass.

'Shall we say – because I like you, my dear Oakshott,' he purred. 'And I liked you on sight.'

So far as Oakshott was concerned they made a frigid parting. He, aware that he was out of his depth in a web of intrigue that promised to stretch from the palace in which he stood to Pitt's office in Whitehall, to Bonaparte in Paris, and heaven knows where else, could only see himself as a small fragment of humanity who had been caught up in a monstrous international conspiracy, a game of bluff and double bluff, of which he had not even been told the basic ground rules. And it left him with a deep unease.

'We shall meet again, Oakshott,' said Bernstorff, taking his hand and retaining it longer than necessary – to Oakshott's distaste. 'You will, of course, keep your own counsel about what I have revealed to you tonight. This in the interests of your own country.' He smiled. 'I will not even insult you by asking for your assurances on this point.

'Farewell, Lord Charles.'

'Your servant, Count Axel.' With a stiff nod of the head.

Oakshott was keenly sensitive that the other's single eye was fixed upon his back all the way to the door. He, who endured without flinching the vagaries of sea and wind, not to mention the violence of his country's enemies, gave an involuntary shudder when he had closed the door behind him.

The same lackey who had guided him through the labyrinth of the royal palace was waiting at a discreet distance down the corridor to lead him back to the reception chamber.

Pepe greeted him upon his return. With the Iberian-Moor were Riou and Bolton. Said Riou: 'Oakshott, I've just come from the admiral. There have been talks tonight, and they've gone badly. It's thought that a discreet withdrawal to our ships would be in order.'

'That's bad news,' said Oakshott.

'Yes,' said Riou. 'It seems that the crown prince, who was chairing the discussion, appeared somewhat distraught.'

'Wouldn't *you*?' drawled Bolton, 'if your father, the king, whom you'd pushed forward to add a little tone to the proceedings, had made such an exhibition of himself?'

'In any event,' said Riou, 'both the admiral and Lord Whitworth were very impressed with the RN turn-out tonight, and asked me to convey their appreciation. There will be another meeting tomorrow apparently, and upon the result of that we shall have to await events.'

'And if the meeting fails to come to a satisfactory conclusion?' asked Oakshott.

'Then the squadron will probably remain here till it does,' said Riou. He looked over his shoulder to ensure that he was not overheard and, lowering his voice, added: 'Or, reinforced by the rest of the fleet, it's likely that we shall attack – and take – Copenhagen!'

Carriages a-plenty were waiting outside the palace to convey the British back to the quay, where ships of the squadron had been ordered to have boats waiting at all hours. Oakshott and Pepe Lopez were rowed back to *Javelin* in their own jollyboat. Wrapped in their cloaks against the dank night air, they looked back to the receding shore lights.

'As to the mysterious lady,' said Pepe, apropos of nothing, 'after you had joined the line to be presented to the king, sir, I observed her leaving on the arm of one of the Danish officers. Upon discreet inquiry, I learned that he was one Admiral Moltke. Her husband, perhaps?'

'Maybe,' growled Oakshott.

'You absented yourself for quite a while, sir. I had thought that, perhaps, you had encountered the lady, after all.'

They were passing close to the Trekroner forts. A voice hailed them from above, and a bullseye lantern was directed to the jollyboat, playing upon the White Ensign which, by order of the admiral, had to be carried by all boats day and night. The lantern was presently extinguished.

'Would you believe that I met none other than Count Bernstorff?' said Oakshott.

'Indeed, sir?' replied Pepe Lopez, surprised.

'And I can tell you this, Pepe,' said Oakshott. 'That gamble you had in mind concerning the person who was instrumental in saving me from court martial . . .'

'Yes, sir?' Eagerly.

'You would have won your wager.

'And I can tell you no more.'

Javelin lay at anchor for more than two weeks, swinging round and round a buoy with the fickle wind – a condition that many sailors declared to be the best part of the seafaring life. During that time the crew enjoyed fresh water, fish, meat, and soft tommy (newly-baked bread) instead of ship's biscuit.

After twenty bland days, enlivened by officers and lower-deck ratings exchanging visits with other ships of the squadron – since the political situation was such that shore leave was out of the question – Oakshott had another call from the admiral's exquisite flag lieutenant. Walker brought with him two sealed packets, one of which *Javelin*'s captain was to open, and act upon its contents with no delay. The other was to be delivered to the addressee, whose identity was contained within Oakshott's instructions.

As soon as Lieutenant Walker was over the side, Oakshott opened his missive and read the contents, contingent upon which he summoned all his officers to attend him in his stern cabin forthwith.

They came. Settled themselves down on a row of chairs which captain's servant Bantock had arranged along the length of the dining table, facing Oakshott, who sat alone on the other side, his back to the sloping stern windows which, at that particular state of the tide, presented a panorama of Copenhagen under a brilliant August sun.

Oakshott eyed them all, running his gaze along the row of faces, some familiar as brothers in arms of long standing, others as yet untried in day-to-day acquaintance in the narrow confines of a war vessel, or in battle. His markedly arithmetical mind discerned a subtractive quality.

'Are we all present?' he asked.

Lieutenant Shacklock answered, speaking as officer-of-the-day: 'Cobbold's adrift, sir,' he said with a note of disfavour. 'Been in his hammock all day. Says he's sick.'

'Has Henshawe seen him?' asked Oakshott. *Javelin* did not carry a ship's surgeon; as in three of Oakshott's previous commissions, this arcane art was discharged by the same veteran ship's carpenter.

'I passed the word for Henshawe to attend him, sir,' said Shacklock, with something like a sneer on his finely-sculpted lips.

Shacklock, thought Oakshott, was the ill-favoured young midshipman who had been with him on his first command. And as unpromising a grubby, mean, snivelling, unwashed specimen of a naval officer as one would go a long way to find; now metamorphosed by the glorious hand of Nature into the preening male creature whom he saw before him; surely destined for admiralcy if his wild courage did not take him first; wearer of the Nile medal which he had won with notable distinction; and terror of grubby, mean, snivelling, unwashed midshipmen like the missing Cobbold. Nature certainly was a wonderful thing.

'Well, then we must proceed with difficulty without Mr Cobbold,' said Oakshott, and took advantage of the slight titter of amusement that followed his sally by running his eye over his orders.

In the silence that followed, he began: 'Gentlemen, we are for Russia.'

'Russia!'

'By God!' The atmosphere sparkled like St Elmo's Fire.

Oakshott nodded. 'My orders are to proceed with all speed and by my best course, to the Russian port of Narva on the Baltic sea, and there to deliver sealed dispatches to His Majesty's Consul in that port, a certain Mr Constantinopolous who, for reasons best known to himself, is of the Greek persuasion.'

The ripple of laughter that followed Oakshott's mild quip was broken by First Lieutenant Brewster.

'Are we provided with charts of the Baltic, sir?' was his question.

'We are not, Mr Brewster,' responded Oakshott. 'We have, as you know, certain *drawings* dating back from the last century, which, though handsomely embellished with naked putti puffing their cheeks mightily and such representations of sea monsters as only landsmen can imagine, hardly suit our need. However, there is a sketch map attached to my orders which informs us that Narva lies close by the Russian capital of St Petersburg and five hundred miles from here as the crow flies on a nor'easterly course on the prevailing wind, so I do not doubt but that we shall make a good landfall – with the help of whatever local knowledge we meet with along the way. Any questions?'

'Are the French in the Baltic, sir?' This from one of the junior lieutenants – Bishop, a Suffolk man.

'From my information, they almost certainly are,' replied Oakshott. 'In any event, we will proceed as if we are sailing in enemy waters, as – no sooner do we have Denmark behind us – we might just as well be.'

There were no other questions. No doubts. No fears. Conscious that *Javelin* was to become a probing finger at the end of the long arm of the Royal Navy, and this in a strange and enclosed sea at a time of perilously shifting allegiances, the ship's officers were soberly aware that there were none like them.

'Sir, I do be grieviously concerned about young Mr Cobbold.'

Pipes were shrilling, bosun's mates were shouting orders across the upper deck. A team of the duty watch was toiling round the capstan, and all hands were aloft at the sails.

Oakshott paused in his restless pacing up and down the quarter-deck to regard Ship's Carpenter Henshawe with whom, though he would never have acknowledged it, he had more in common than any other man in the ship.

'What's wrong with him, Henshawe?' he asked.

'Well, it do seem that the young gennleman did have a fall from the mizzen chains when we wuz shortening sail a week or so back, sir,' said the Geordie. 'He fell atop of a gun carriage and took a nasty cut high up in the thigh. Didn't say much about it to anyone, but carried on with his duties uncomplaining like.'

'And now?' demanded Oakshott.

'Now, sir,' said *Javelin*'s acting unpaid surgeon extraordinary, 'I do think that he is taken of the fever from his wound as might shortly repose him to Abraham's bosom, sir.'

Oakshott looked about him. The capstan party had

brought the anchor up and down; it needed only a quarter of an hour, at most, with the wind still veering, before they need get under way.

'Take me to him, Henshawe,' said Oakshott.

The midshipmen's gun room was a narrow half of the gun deck just abaft of the beam. In it the four young subordinate officers of the ship's complement lived and had their being. It was dark, bare and uncomfortable, and stank vilely of feet.

One hammock, alone, swung gently with the rise and fall of the ship in the middle of the space. In it lay Midshipman Cobbold, asleep or unconscious, an unhealthy flush suffusing the cheekbones of his normally pale countenance.

Gently Henshawe drew aside the blanket that covered the boy's lower limbs. Oakshott drew breath sharply, to observe a cruel gash that marked the inner thigh of the right leg, high up.

'You do see, sir,' said Henshawe, pointing, 'as how the young gennleman were nigh to being deprived of his particulars. That be a nasty wound, caused – as well as I can figure – by a pricker what some slovenly gun captain did leave standing up in the touch-hole of the gun in question.'

'And what now, Henshawe?' asked Oakshott, already composing in his mind the terms of the letter of condolence that he might shortly be penning to the boy's unfortunate mother. 'He is feverish, as I observe? Will it take him off? Is the wound gangrenous?'

He took a closer look at the gash on the unconscious boy's naked thigh, and recoiled in horror.

'By God, Henshawe!' he exclaimed. '*The damned wound's alive and crawling with maggots!*'

'And best remain so, sir,' responded the other with some complacency.

'What are you saying, man?' demanded Oakshott.

'They little demons, sir,' said Henshawe, actually touching the discernibly bloated larvae that squirmed and wriggled within the red maw of the festering wound, 'be giving the young gennleman the best aid that can be had. The maggot, sir, now he do not eat of 'ealthy flesh, but only of dead flesh. Better than all the medicines in the world be a colony o' lively, hungry maggots, what will eat away the bad parts and leave the young gennleman's wound as clean and wholesome as you'd please.*

'All we have to worry for, sir, is that the fever don't take him first.'

'I devoutly hope you're right, Henshawe,' said Oakshott.

'So do I, sir,' responded the other, 'for 'tis a sad thing to see so young a lad taken so cruelly early.'

A shrilling of pipes signalled Oakshott that the wind was favourable. He went up on deck to watch his ship get under way.

'Three sail to the nor'ard, sir!'

Oakshott had slept badly, and the excited summons, delivered by the midshipman of the watch in the dawn light, dragging him from an inconclusive dream concerning Irene Chancellor, did little to soften his awakening.

'Beat to quarters,' he said, reaching for his boat cloak.

'Done, sir!' came the response, as the sound of pipes and kettle drums resounded through the ship.

The guns were being run out as Oakshott won the upper deck and was immediately drenched by an influx of spindrift as the ship went over on another tack.

Shacklock was on watch. Obedient to captain's standing orders, he had immediately turned the ship towards the newcomers, presuming them to be enemy. Oakshott nodded approval, just as Brewster showed his head above the companionway.

'Closed up and ready for action, sir!' he reported.

*Oddly, modern clinicians have come up with some evidence to support this theory of *Javelin*'s amateur surgeon.

'Very good, Number One.'

'They're Froggies, sir!' This from the masthead. 'Two frigates and one as looks like a sloop.'

'We'll take them on,' said Oakshott.

'Issue pistols and cutlasses, sir?' asked Shacklock, making no attempt to keep the eagerness from his voice.

'No – there'll be no question of boarding, no matter how it goes,' said Oakshott, 'for our first duty is to reach Narva with the dispatches. I propose to stand off and engage them singly, Mr Shacklock. Maintain your present course.'

'Aye, aye, sir!'

Oakshott had scarcely been on deck for five minutes before the ever attentive Bantock was up with a mug of steaming cocoa laced with rum. *Javelin*'s captain took it gratefully, and sipped as he looked about him, weighing up his chances in the coming encounter.

About ten miles astern, and clear in the dawn light, was the Baltic island of Gotland – so named on the vestigial charts which were at hand. They had passed close by it during the first watch and observed lights ashore. About a hundred and fifty miles to the north, the Baltic bifurcated into the Gulf of Bothnia to port and the Gulf of Finland to starboard. Narva lay within the latter.

And between *Javelin* and her landfall – three Frenchmen!

'They're big fellows, the frigates – thirty-sixes or thirty-eights!'

Eager young eyes were feeding Oakshott with information.

The men grouped on the quarter-deck watched him questioningly.

'What I shall do,' said Oakshott, 'is to make a feint for the lead ship and back off as soon as we come within range. We have the weather gauge, so she will be out of the battle for all the time it takes for her to turn about and tack back. That should give us enough time for a brief pounding match with number two. Mind you, gentlemen,' he added, 'there'll be no wild heroics this morning. Bear in mind that our first duty is to carry the dispatch to Narva.'

It was a good and simple plan, aggressive and well considered; typical of the philosophy that was current in the new Georgian navy due to the influence of Horatio Nelson and others. At the heart of it was the audacity of putting a superior force at a disadvantage.

'The sloop's turning away, sir!'

Oakshott aimed his glass. The enemy sloop, third in the line – and it was a bad and ragged line at that – had tacked away to port and was getting clear of the coming encounter. This accorded with the general practice of minor vessels of war avoiding action when heavily outgunned.

'All guns load,' said Oakshott.

The order was carried down to the gundeck through a speaking trumpet by First Lieutenant Brewster in the unmistakable accent of the Commonwealth of Massachusetts. The response was an immediate cacophony, rapidly culminating with the response: *'Ready to fire!'*

At half a mile distance from the French, *Javelin* was running free under plain sail in a stiff wind. The enemy was sailing close-hauled on the starboard tack with the lead ship almost dead ahead; indeed, Oakshott, with plenty of scope with the wind behind him, ordered his quartermaster to steer on a collision course.

The range closed, and the advantage – as things stood – clearly lay with the French with every closing yard, for the enemy leader could now bring a broadside to bear on the Englishman, and his consort would soon do likewise. On the other hand, though pointing straight at the enemy with none of her guns bearing, *Javelin* presented only a narrow target.

If Oakshott was aware that his companions on the quarter-deck were stealing anxious glances towards him as the distance lessened with each passing moment, he did not show it, but slowly paced to and fro, telescope tucked under his arm, hands loosely clasped behind his back.

'The leader's opened fire, sir!'

A blossoming of white gunsmoke from amidships revealed that the enemy had discharged one gun.

'It's a ranging shot,' said *Javelin*'s imperturbable captain. 'Well, we shall see what we shall see.'

Seconds later, a pillar of white water was kicked up twenty yards ahead of *Javelin*'s long bowsprit.

'That was most obliging of him,' murmured Oakshott. 'I'll make that my turning mark.' And, loudly, to the quartermaster: 'Port your helm!'

The lean frigate bowed grandly as she turned to port, and kept turning – turning – till she was sailing parallel with the French line *and on a completely opposite course.*

'Steady as you go!' ordered Oakshott. 'All guns stand by to open fire in succession as your targets bear!'

Javelin and the lead Frenchman were now abreast. The latter essayed a ragged broadside, but Oakshott held his fire, and was gratified to see that the other's shots were still falling short.

A few moments later, when Oakshott's calculating mind had fixed the precise geometry of the manoeuvre, he gave another order: 'Starboard your helm. Shape course to pass under his stern!'

The boldness, the simplicity of the manoeuvre, were immediately apparent to everyone on the quarter-deck with him – though the import may have evaded the French, who almost certainly surmised that the Englishman was merely coming in to close the range for an exchange of broadsides. After all – the leader's consort was sailing in her wake with less than a hundred yards separating the two ships. The notion of cutting the enemy line with such a narrow margin for success would not have occurred to one captain in a thousand.

Oakshott was just such a captain – and his men knew it.

*

Doubtless secure in their minds about the strength of their disposition and the overwhelming weight of shot that lay at their command, the French maintained their course, and *Javelin* drew nearer. As she passed beyond the leader's beam, and came under fire from her after guns, a considerable amount of shot came inboard, but the aiming was high. A peppering of holes was punched through the mains and topsails, some cordage was cut away, a few spars fractured. One 24-pound ball struck the coaming close by the foremast and the shower of splintered elm daggered to death a topman who was hauling on a line.

Then they were past the other's stern, and Oakshott, silent in the din, pointed the course for the helmsmen to follow: he need scarcely have troubled – the quartermaster had discerned his captain's intent to an inch. He and his two brawny assistants bore down on the great wheel, and *Javelin*'s bowsprit turned to pass under the Frenchman's counter with no more than a pistol shot separating them.

'Give fire!'

As the guns of the starboard battery came to bear in succession upon the enemy's carved and gilded counter they fired at point-blank range. From where he was standing Oakshott saw a line of stern windows punched right through. He saw the ship's name – it was *Eloise* – limned upon an ornamental cartouche in raised and enamelled letters: it disappeared from his gaze.

Sixteen guns emptied themselves into the luckless *Eloise*.

And then *Javelin* was through – having broken the enemy line.

It now remained for the port battery to turn their fury upon the second in line, who, observing the Englishman's intent, was beginning a turn which would bring a broadside to bear. Before the manoeuvre had scarcely begun, *Javelin*'s guns spoke out again, and the fore part of the Frenchman – bowsprit, foremast, fo'c's'le and galley – took a terrible punishment.

'And that, gentlemen,' declared Oakshott, 'is it! Break off the action. Our duty now lies elsewhere. Hard a starboard!'

As *Javelin* heeled sharply to starboard, the second Frenchman contrived to get off a half broadside and some of the shots came inboard. There were cries of wounded in the gundeck below, but these were soon drowned by a ragged cheer that began on the quarter-deck and spread over the ship.

'The Frog's afire!'

Oakshott halted in his striding and aimed his telescope. Quite clearly, from the shattered fo'c's'le of their last adversary, a column of black smoke was being whipped away in the wind, and a tongue of orange-yellow flame was licking at the heads.

'By Jove, she is, sir,' said Shacklock at his elbow. 'Do you suppose that the Frogs didn't even trouble to douse the galley fire when they went into action?'

'If they did not, then they'll be very sorry,' opined Oakshott. 'That fire's gaining fast.'

On her best point of sail, *Javelin* was soon speeding away from the scene of this brisk action, nor did either of the enemy frigates attempt to give chase. Of the sloop there was no sign.

Brewster came aft. The first lieutenant's elongated countenance was powder-blackened. After him came Henshawe, ship's carpenter and amateur surgeon.

'What was the butcher's bill, Number One?'

'One topman killed and put overboard, sir,' was the response. 'Six gunners wounded and two of them like to die – according to Henshawe, here.'

Oakshott cocked a questioning eye at the latter.

'That be so, in my opinion, sir,' confirmed the amateur surgeon. 'On the credit side, as you might say, howsomever, young Mr Cobbold, he be on the mend. They little demons has cleaned his wound and the fever have abated.'

'Well, that's a consolation,' said Oakshott. He looked about him, to where the crewmen were already clearing away the debris of the encounter: reeving fresh ropes that had been severed, swabbing the powder swarf from the white decks. Two of Henshawe's assistants were hard at work putting in a fresh piece of fine seasoned elm where the French ball had taken away the coaming with a fatal result.

'The ship's done well in that little encounter, Number One,' mused *Javelin*'s captain. 'And it's to be hoped that the native Balts come to hear of our exploit and take it into account if or when they consider throwing in their lot with Bonaparte.

'I think, under the circumstances, Number One . . .'

'Yes, sir?'

Oakshott saw Henshawe moisten his lips in anticipation.

'Splice the main-brace, if you please.'

Part Three

KATERINA

SEVEN

That hot August, the winds failed them off the mouth of the Gulf of Finland. *Javelin* wallowed for days in light airs within sight of the islands off the Estonian shore to the south-west, and the crew amused themselves by fishing over the side. To their disappointment, not to say disgust, they soon discovered that the low salinity of the Baltic did not support the sort of plump herrings they were used to enjoy off Harwich or Plymouth; instead, they had to be content with little fellows a fifth of the size, more like sardines – but excellent as to taste nevertheless.

Oakshott watched the fishing with approval, knowing as he did the great importance of keeping an idle crew not only employed but also amused.

'Shall we be long in Narva, sir?' asked Brewster, who himself was trailing a fishing line over the transom.

'My orders are to hand over the dispatches to our Mr Constantinopolous and remain in the port under his direction,' replied Oakshott. 'Presumably to be on hand, to carry any vital news back to our masters. It's to be hoped,' he added, 'that our stay is not too much protracted. According to the best information I have, the ports of the Gulf of Finland are closed by ice for as much as three or four months of the year, and I have no wish to Christmas in an ice-bound port in *ultima Thule*.'

The American nodded agreement, and remarked how the

once glassy sea was beginning to form wavelets, and that *Javelin*'s sagging sails were shaking themselves out like lines of washing.

That evening, the frigate was heading into the gulf on a fresh southerly breeze.

They came upon the port of Narva after skirting a steep shoreline that rose level upon level, set with pine forests in which nestled small villages and hamlets built mostly of wood, with onion-domed churches. Taking careful soundings all the way, they found plenty of water, and it was during the afternoon watch that Oakshott was called on deck at the sighting of the entrance to the port and town which, in accordance with such charts and sketch maps as the ship possessed, were dominated by two ancient fortresses on the east bank and west bank of the Narva river.

There were small craft – coasters, fishing boats and such – moving in and out of the port. The wind having veered to the west, to their advantage, Oakshott accordingly decided to enter the river forthwith, following the main stream of craft and taking continuous soundings.

Presently, the last loop of the river brought them to a sizeable inland lake where the main part of the town rose on gentle slopes to left and right. It was there – two cables distant from a busy quay, that *Javelin* dropped anchor.

'Fire a salute for a sovereign state,' ordered Oakshott. 'And dress overall.'

Every flag in the ship was being strung from bowsprit to taffrail as the port battery facing the nearer shore loaded without shot and proceeded to discharge a salute of twenty-one guns from fore to aft, the first five pieces reloading to fire twice.

'Well, sir,' said Brewster, 'that should have caused a clatter in the pigeon loft.'

'Boat putting out from shore and approaching, sir!'

'Pass the word for my secretary to come on deck,' said Oakshott.

The boat, a type of four-oared cutter, appeared to be carrying a passenger in the stern sheets. Though the craft was still some distance away, Oakshott, steadying his telescope on the shoulder of the midshipman-of-the-watch, managed to make out that the passenger appeared to be a personage of considerable *embonpoint* and distinctly Levantine appearance, who was carrying a parasol against the afternoon sun.

'If I am not mistaken, we are about to have a visit from our Mr Constantinopolous,' said Oakshott, addressing the officer of the day. 'So we will accord him the honours of a ship's captain.'

'Aye, aye, sir.'

As the boat drew close, Oakshott found no cause to alter his first summation of the newcomer. Nor was he mistaken. When, after some difficulty, the boat's crew managed to assist their portly passenger on to *Javelin*'s deck, and he was greeted with a Piping of the Side, his smiling countenance was turned upon Oakshott and he announced himself in unaccented English:

'Alexandros Constantinopolous, His Britannic Majesty's Consul-General in Narva and province. At your service, Captain – ah? . . .'

'Oakshott. Welcome aboard *Javelin*, sir. May I present my officers . . .'

Introductions over, the Greek switched facial masks from amiability to deadly seriousness. He took Oakshott by the elbow and, leading him to the other side of the deck, breathed into his ear.

'It is imperative that I see you alone, Captain. The matter will brook no delay, and is of the highest importance.'

'Of course.' There being no need of an interpreter, Oakshott dismissed Pepe Lopez and the officers with a nod and a glance, and led his guest below to the stern cabin.

There, while Constantinopolous settled himself in an easy chair and the other poured them glasses of madeira, Oakshott was able to make a rough appraisal of his visitor.

Clad in a watered silk coat of brilliant green that put any of First Lieutenant Brewster's to shame, a flowered waistcoat in which a vast paunch sagged, his surprisingly well-formed legs encased in white pantaloons, the figure suggested a lifetime of indulgent living. The head, crowned with black wavy hair into which the iron had surely entered, and the multiplicity of chins, seemed to confirm this. It was only when one regarded the eyes – black as night, deeply set, shrewd and humorous – and the mobile mouth set above a firm jaw – that one was inclined to think again.

Decidedly a character to be reckoned with, thought Oakshott.

'I thank you, sir,' said the consul, taking his glass and pledging his host. 'I trust you had a good passage. I was apprised of the coming of a fast ship.' He took an appreciative sip of his wine. 'And now – to business.

'To understand the situation here,' he said, setting down his glass, 'you must know that there has been a grave turn in the events following Lord Whitworth's diplomatic endeavours in Copenhagen. The Tsar Paul, who is hell-bent to throw in Russia's lot with Bonaparte, has called upon Denmark, Sweden, and Prussia to unite with him in establishing an Armed Neutrality which is to be exactly what its name implies: absolute freedom on the high seas – *or war with England!*'

'And why has the tsar conceived such a hatred for us?' asked Oakshott.

'The key is Malta,' replied the Greek. 'As you may know, Paul has been made Grand Master of the Knights of St John, an appointment which, in the fullness of time, he aims to translate into his sovereignty of Malta.'

'But – Bonaparte captured Malta, and the French are still there!' said Oakshott. And then, after a moment's thought and a glance from the shrewd eyes opposite him, he added, '*Ahh! . . .*'

'Exactly!' said Constantinopolous. 'The British fleet is investing Malta, and the island will fall at any time. Paul knows that Bonaparte might be persuaded to accommodate him – at a price – but that once the British set foot on Malta, there they will stay!'

They were silent for a while, and Oakshott was uncomfortably aware that he was being regarded, and appraised, with the same keen scrutiny as that to which he had lately submitted his guest.

Presently, the Greek continued: 'Which brings me to my reason for coming aboard your ship without delay, Captain. It is simply this – in anticipation of the British taking Malta, the Tsar issued an edict the day before yesterday – *by which all British property within the dominions of the Russian state is sequestered!*'

'I see now why I was sent here,' said Oakshott. 'My masters anticipated such a move. I am to return immediately with the news.' He felt curiously lightened at the prospect, for the notion of being holed up for the winter in an icebound port had been haunting his dreams of late.

Alas for prospects . . .

'That will not be necessary, Captain,' said Constantinopolous. 'By good fortune there chanced to be one of our allies – a fast Dutch merchantman – leaving for London river on the day that I received the news of the sequestrations, and her captain was happy to carry my dispatch. No, sir, you must remain here to convey what, I am convinced, will be even graver news when the British take Malta – as they most certainly must, and soon.'

'And what will that be, sir?' asked Oakshott, who thought that he knew the answer.

'That Holy Russia has thrown in her lot with Godless

France, sir,' came the reply, 'and declared war on Great Britain!'

Oakshott recharged their glasses, noting with surprise that his hand was trembling slightly with what he assumed to be excitement.

'I thank you, sir,' said the consul. 'When that news arrives – and I have agents in the province who will bring it to me in good, safe time – I shall wish you to convey me and my staff to England so that I can give my appreciation of the situation to Mr Pitt himself. Do I make myself clear?'

'Perfectly, sir,' responded *Javelin*'s captain.

'One more matter before I leave, Captain Oakshott,' said the Greek. 'There is a personage of great influence who has a villa here in Narva. Her name is Baroness Jacobson, widow of an Estonian diplomat who once held high office at the Court of St Petersburg. A much-travelled lady, the baroness is intensely pro-English. In my capacity as consul-general, I am well received at the Villa Jacobson and never decline an invitation there, however pressing my personal affairs.' His shrewd, black eyes twinkled up at Oakshott with a certain – was it defensiveness? The latter thought he discerned by what means this outwardly unprepossessing man had risen – from whatever Levantine marketplace undoubtedly represented his humble beginnings – to his present eminence.

'Indeed,' murmured Oakshott.

'I mentioned to the baroness that I was expecting the arrival of a Royal Naval frigate and she expressed an interest.' He tapped Oakshott's arm. 'She is extremely hospitable. Should she extend an invitation to you and your officers to visit her, accept without hesitation. It will be greatly to our mutual interests.' He winked, extended his hand for Oakshott to take, and shook it warmly.

On their way on to the upper deck, Oakshott inquired of his departing guest if the tsar's edict of sequestration was causing any repercussions in the port.

'Most appallingly!' replied the consul. 'Why, there are British merchants in plenty in Narva. They are my principal interest. They own warehouses, quays, docks. Naturally, they have homes - many of them prosperous homes. In the last few days, sir, I have been swamped - *swamped* - with them crowding to my office, demanding to know where they stand, how they can continue to live and work under the threat that hangs above them. A few have already started to negotiate for the sale of their interests and to return home. But who will buy - when, by waiting till the tsar's edict is enforced in a few days' time, any Russian subject will be able to pick up a going concern from the tsar's commissioners for a few paltry roubles?

'It is a bad business, Captain Oakshott, and it will get worse.' He lowered his voice as they came within earshot of the officers and watchkeepers on the gangway. 'But more of that later, sir. Be prepared, I beg you, to make sail back to England at - say - twelve hours' notice.'

Oakshott promised that he would.

They piped the consul over the side to his waiting boat, and Oakshott watched him go.

'To think,' murmured Shacklock, who held foreigners - all foreigners - in no very high regard, 'that that great greasy bladder of lard represents *us* abroad!'

'You are mistaken, Mr Shacklock,' responded Oakshott, who had overheard the aside. 'Unless *I* am mistaken, there goes a man - a mere pawn in the great affairs of Europe - who will survive, by some means or other, long after Bonaparte, the tsar, and half the generals and admirals have been swept from the board!'

That evening, a message was brought by bum-boat addressed to Captain Lord Charles Oakshott RN, Commanding Officer, HMS *Javelin*. It was sealed with a wafer bearing a coat of arms of continental appearance, and the address was penned in a slanting, female hand.

Oakshott broke the seal and opened the missive with some surprise. But why should he be surprised? he asked himself. The wily Greek consul-general had predicted an invitation, and here it was . . .

Katerina, Baroness Jacobson requests the pleasure of Captain Lord Charles Oakshott's company to supper tomorrow evening, Friday, at 7 of the clock. A carriage will await Lord Charles at the end of the pier, to convey him to the Villa Jacobson. RSVP by the messenger.

No mention of bringing his officers. Was this then to be an affair for only high-ups, or – an odd thought – was it to be a supper *à deux*? An intriguing notion, Oakshott!

Without more ado, he wrote a similarly formal note of acceptance and sent it up to be given to the waiting bumboatman.

At the close of the first dog watch the following day, Oakshott, clad in his dress coat, new nankeen breeches and silk stockings, gold-buckled pumps, dress sword on hip and Nile medal at the throat, took a last look at himself in the mirror held up by his servant Bantock.

'Mmm – I wonder – is this coat getting rather shabby, do you think, Bantock?'

'The faded gold braid do add a certain distinction, sir,' said the other with the air of someone repeating a well-learned lesson. 'And good material never does look shabby – only interestingly mature. I should know, for wasn't my father a master tailor?'

'Mmmm.'

'Jollyboat alongside, sir.' From the door.

'Very good.'

Oakshott was rowed to shore in the ship's ten-oared jolly-boat, with the evening sunshine touching every wavelet and reflecting from the spires and domes of the city beyond the dockland. The pier jutted out from a busy part of the quayside, where flotillas of fishing craft lay huddled alongside the wall like baby whales nestling to the mother.

The boat's crew tossed oars and the midshipman brought his craft neatly to the steps at the end of the pier, where several idle hands among the loafers gathered there willingly took their lines and made them fast.

'Return to the ship,' said Oakshott. 'I'll hire a boat to bring me offshore.'

'Aye, aye, sir.'

A glance at his watch confirmed what a clock tower at the inboard end of the pier announced: it was seven precisely.

'Is Milord Oakshott?' The speaker wore a livery of dark brown with silver frogging. He saluted Oakshott and directed him to a two-horse carriage which had been part-hidden by an inquisitive crowd about it. Bowing, the coachman opened the door for the tall figure in alien uniform and Oakshott was driven away – to the wide-eyed speculation of the onlookers.

The route led through a medieval part of the town, a district of streets so narrow that the eaves nearly touched overhead, and past the rampart walls of a massive fortress that must have been old when King Alfred ruled in Wessex. From there the road snaked through a pine forest for a mile or so, ever mounting, till it emerged at length in a clearing where stood a delightful building designed in the rococo style much favoured in the middle of the previous century: a place of subtle delicacy with a hint of pleasant decadence in its slightly overburdened charm.

The carriage drew up at the foot of twin, curving steps that led up to the entrance porch. Two footmen, both in the brown and silver livery, opened the door, lowered the step and assisted Oakshott to alight. He was then bidden, by gestures, to follow them.

The entrance hall of the Villa Jacobson was roofed by a dome, the underside of which was embellished with a convoluted mural painting in the French manner, representing nymphs and satyrs disporting themselves in bosky woodlands. The floor was tiled in a chequerboard of blue and white, to match the colours of the delicately filigreed walls of fine plasterwork.

'Milord . . .'

The footmen took stand on either side of open double doors at the end of the hall and bowed, motioning Oakshott to enter, which he did, and the doors were closed behind him.

Immediately, he was struck with a sense of familiarity, of having passed that way before, the feeling that something predictable was about to happen, the notion that he was in the presence of someone whom he had encountered on more than one occasion . . .

'Lord Charles – how nice to meet you.'

She was seated – or, rather, was half-reclining – in a chaise longue to his right, just beyond the range of his vision, so that he had to turn to regard her.

Her hair was ice-blonde and untouched by powder. Her perfect face had the colouring of pink and white porcelain that surely owed nothing to artifice.

'I am Katerina Jacobson,' she said, extending a white-gloved hand. 'Your Consul, the egregious Constantinopolous, was here to tea yesterday after going aboard your ship. He told me all about you.' Her blue eyes – deep blue like lapis lazuli – held acres of mystery.

Oakshott took her hand. A doubt as light as thistledown that had clouded his mind following her opening phrases was blown away. Now there was no doubt – no doubt at all . . .

'Baroness, we have met before,' he said.

'Indeed?' She seemed amused.

'And you have had knowledge of me before Constantinopolous.'

Her smile was piquant, slightly lop-sided, causing a dimple to appear in her smooth right cheek. She pillowed her chin in her hand and continued to gaze steadily up at him.

'How do you deduce that, sir?' she asked.

'Why, ma'am, you addressed me, both now and in your invitation by my courtesy title.'

She shrugged her slender shoulders, bare above the white Grecian shift of wild white silk.

'And why should I not?' she asked. 'I had it from the consul.'

'With respect, you did not, ma'am,' said Oakshott.

His small dart struck its mark. The faintest indentation of a frown appeared on her placid brow.

'How is that, sir?' she demanded.

Oakshott let a few moments pass, fixing her expression in his mind, so that he was in a position to observe the slightest change that his declaration might bring.

'Because, ma'am, when I introduced myself to Mr Constantinopolous, I used the simple styling of "Captain Oakshott", *tout court*. It is my customary practice with foreigners - even those who appear to be well acquainted with England and the English - so that they do not mistakenly suppose me to be a peer.'

Silence. His revelation brought not the slightest change of expression to that perfect countenance.

And then she began to laugh. 'Sir, you have caught me out in my small deception,' she said at length, her eyes challenging him to pursue his probing - or so it seemed to Oakshott.

'May I hazard the guess that we last exchanged glances at the reception in the Christiansborg Palace, Copenhagen, not very many weeks ago?' he murmured.

She smiled and nodded, the dimple appearing again.

'And before that – in London?'

Another nod.

'This, at a public place of entertainment, though of impeccable respectability – indeed, my sister-in-law was once employed as a singer there, and she an archdeacon's daughter – called Mogg's Diversions?'

'Yes, I think I was there,' she said. She tapped the end of the chaise longue. 'Sit down beside me.'

He obeyed, and was immediately and disturbingly made aware of her nearness, her warmth, the scent of her.

Oakshott cleared his throat and marshalled his thoughts as well as he was able before her disconcerting gaze. 'I must say, ma'am,' he essayed, 'that I find the conjunction of circumstances of our meetings most – coincidental. Indeed, I would say that there is coincidence here as would be quite unacceptable in a work of polite fiction, to say the least.'

She nodded, leaned forward and tapped him on the wrist, gently, with her fan. 'You are quite right, sir,' she said. 'And I will enlighten you as to this series of – coincidences.

'The nub of it is this: I was at both of these places – London and Copenhagen – in company with my brother. And it is no mystery why he should have been in either – since both your interests and his coincide to a considerable degree.'

'Your brother, ma'am?' asked Oakshott, surprised. 'Do I know this gentleman, then?'

'You do – he is Axel Bernstorff.'

'Bernstorff!'

Oakshott had been right in the wilder of his two guesses; this was no gathering of the highly placed and distinguished. When a major-domo tapped upon the door and entered, intimating to his mistress that all was ready, and she took

Oakshott's arm and guided him into the adjoining room, he saw a candlelit table laid for two.

He took his seat facing hers across the small, oval table. The candlelight played marvellously with her features, her colouring, the delicate structure of her shoulders and bosom. They did not speak till they had been served an iced fish soup – an enterprise that called for the attendance of three servitors apiece.

'We may speak freely together in English,' said Katerina Jacobson when she had tasted the first spoonful with all the delicacy and delight of a kitten trying a saucer of cream. 'The servants won't understand a word.'

'Is your brother, the count, here with you also in Narva, ma'am?'

'No, he is not,' she replied. 'He was still in Copenhagen when I left soon after the reception at the Christiansborg – no doubt adding his weight to the diplomatic negotiations after his usual fashion.'

'And his usual fashion is? . . .' Oakshott left the question in the air.

She smiled and laid aside her spoon. 'I think you have had some small experience of my brother's methods, sir,' she replied. 'Be assured that, in this instance – as in others – his methods will be devious, pragmatic – and no doubt successful.'

'So, he is still in Copenhagen?'

'I think not,' she replied, taking up her spoon again. 'I think that he may be in Paris.'

'Being devious, pragmatic, and no doubt successful, with Bonaparte?'

She did not reply, nor did she speak again till the servants had cleared away the soup and provided them each with a minute roast duckling which, when pierced, emitted a piquant sauce on to one's plate.

'You have formed a – certain opinion – about my brother, no doubt,' she said.

'It was not difficult,' was Oakshott's guarded reply to that.

'Lord Charles, you may be very frank with me,' she said, spearing the tiny carcass before her. 'Axel and I are – have always been – very close. As close as any two siblings can get, even if they are identical twins, which we are not, for he is five years older than I. There are many – and you are surely among them – who find his methods distasteful. I would not blame you on that score, for I regard my brother with both eyes wide and I hold on to him with open hands.

'Axel succeeded to the Bernstorff inheritance, the title, and the limitless fortune that goes with it. For the greater part of his adult life, he was the dissolute rake, notorious in London, Paris, Rome, Vienna. Gambling, womanizing, scandalizing. It was as if he wanted to burn himself out like a meteor, to be snuffed out in the high heavens and not fall to earth with ignominy.

'It was then – during a wild chase across country for a wager – that he had a terrible fall from his horse. For weeks he hung in the limbo between life and death. And when he recovered, he was a changed man. Changed physically by the loss of an eye, and with certain other impediments. But mostly he was changed – within.

'It was as if, during those weeks in limbo, he had had a vision of his greater, fulfilled self. And he knew what it was that he was after.

'That thing – that goal which has driven him on ever since – is the pursuit of power. And by any means!'

As she spoke those words, Oakshott seemed to be transported back to that dimly-lit chamber in the palace at Copenhagen, and he regarding the dark-clad figure striding to and fro, the candlelight making grotesque giant shadows of his gesticulating arms upon the tapestried walls. He seemed to hear that voice ranting with self-adulation of his his power and influence in the courts and chancelleries of power . . .

'I have become the eyes and ears of all Europe!'

Katerina Jacobson was still talking. He regarded her keenly. Not unlike her brother – and yet totally unlike. The same air of total assurance, but in her case it was overlaid and mellowed by the femininity which informed her every glance, every passing gesture.

She was still talking – rhapsodizing about that confounded brother of hers, as he expressed it to himself – as innumerable courses were set before them and removed, largely untouched.

Later, much later, when they were sitting facing each other over their cognac, she smiled at him, and Oakshott was totally bewitched by her.

'I have quite monopolized our conversation,' she said. 'My apologies.'

'Your discourse has been most illuminating,' he replied. 'But something occurred to me while you were talking. Yes, I understand how it came about that both you and your brother were in London and Copenhagen together, and how it was that your brother's interests were intertwined with mine.

'What I cannot understand, however' – he leaned forward across the table towards her and spoke more slowly and with earnestness – 'is how it happened that we should meet, that night, in Mogg's Diversions of all places. Mogg's has nothing to do with your brother's interests, nor for that matter with mine.'

She matched his gravity with her expression.

'Sir,' she said, 'it happened that I was in the Admiralty, waiting for my brother, when I chanced to see you pass out into the night.

'So – I followed after you.'

'Ah!' exclaimed Oakshott, but, still puzzled: 'Why did you do that, ma'am?'

'Lord Charles,' she replied, 'there are some questions which, out of delicacy and concern for a lady's modesty, a gentleman does not ask.'

With these words she drained her glass and, rising, left the table, crossing the room to a small door set in the panelling into which she disappeared, leaving the door part open.

Oakshott shrugged, refilled his glass, and awaited her return.

Five minutes passed. Ten. And still no Katerina Jacobson.

Uneasy, now, and fearful that he had offended her, Oakshott rose and walked over to the door and peered inside.

There was a small chamber. In it a pretty four-poster bed hung with pink and silver draperies. Katerina was standing and regarding herself in a pier glass. As she saw his reflection in the mirror she turned to him with a frown that was not quite a frown.

'You certainly take your time, Captain!' she murmured.

Then she did something with the Grecian shift, upon which it whispered to the floor about her feet.

EIGHT

Oakshott presently managed to secure for *Javelin* one of the greatly coveted berths alongside the quay – but not without some difficulty. Narva was a busy port, taking much of the trading overspill from St Petersburg, and it called for all Oakshott's powers of persuasion – augmented by a case of his best sherry – to convince the harbourmaster, through Pepe Lopez, that it was in the interests of all concerned for him to have immediate access to the Resident British Consul-General; besides, there was the matter of purchasing and taking aboard stores to augment *Javelin*'s dwindling supplies. The harbourmaster had a lien on ships' stores in Narva; it was probably this argument that won the day.

'Have you noticed, Pepe, how the skipper goes ashore most afternoons since we've been alongside the wall?'

'How could one not, Number One? And always dressed up to the nines. Lucky fellow, he.'

Oakshott had just been piped over the gangway. The speakers watched their captain's tall figure disappear in the crowded quayside. In the interests of safety during the present differences with their nominal allies, Oakshott had ordained that no shore leave would be granted.

'Well, it's no use repining,' said Brewster. 'I have to check the gunnery stores.' The American cast a wistful glance towards a pretty chit of a thing with pigtails and flashing eyes who strode past the ship, balancing on her head a basket of fish – and with all the grace of a Greek caryatid. He sighed and went below.

In his progress along the quay Oakshott was not conscious of any signs of hostility, overt or otherwise, from the passing crowds. *Javelin* had been in port long enough for her colours to be recognized, the same with his uniform. Whatever the opinions of Tsar Paul, they were evidently not shared by the majority of his subjects. And then Oakshott remembered that this was not Russia, but Estonia, which the Russkies had won from Sweden in the middle of the last century – on most unfavourable terms for the poor Estonians.

He came to the British consulate, which was a substantial building at the end of the quay with a courtyard in front and a range of stabling and outbuildings to the rear. The Union Flag drooped forlornly over the portico through which Oakshott entered. He was conveyed by one of the consul's functionaries down a long corridor lined on both sides with downcast-looking people, men and women both: British subjects dispossessed by the tsar's edict and seeking help and advice from their own sovereign's representative. It seemed to Oakshott that there were about twice the number that he had encountered there the previous afternoon.

One of the men plucked at his sleeve in passing.

'Captain, I beg you. I am a man of considerable substance, acquainted with Mr Pitt. Will you not convey me and my family back home when you leave? I have money . . .'

'I'm sorry, sir,' murmured Oakshott, disengaging himself.

The consul was sitting in his shirtsleeves and looking much put upon. He sat back in his chair and sighed when his visitor was announced.

'My God, Oakshott, I am at my wit's end,' he declared. 'You saw them out there! Already, I have twelve families occupying the outbuildings, and another three camping in the gardens. What will happen if the situation has not changed when the snows come, I cannot bring myself even to contemplate. Sit down, my dear fellow. Tea?'

'Thank you no, Consul. It's a little early for me. What fresh news, if any?'

Constantinopolous rang a handbell, which brought a boy running, from whom he ordered to be brought a pot of tea. He then re-addressed himself to his visitor.

'My agent in St Petersburg sent word that the tsar has closeted himself in the Summer Palace and sees no one but his own ministers, the Swedish, Danish and Prussian ambassadors – and can you guess who else?' The man's jowls quivered with indignation as his clever eyes searched Oakshott's face for intelligence.

'Some French emissary or other?' said Oakshott, drawing a bow at a venture.

'Quite right!' exclaimed the Greek. 'So you may see which way the wind blows. I think that the tsar will join with Bonaparte within the week. And then we shall have to move swiftly. I only hope that my agent in Petersburg is first here with the news.'

'And Malta?' asked Oakshott.

'No news,' said the other. 'But you may take it, Oakshott, that the fall of Malta is the key, as I have always said.'

'I see that another British merchantman came into the anchorage this morning,' said Oakshott.

'That makes three in all,' said Constantinopolous. 'I have put them at twelve hours' notice for sailing, like yourself. It is my hope that this will give us time to load aboard as many of our people as possible in the four ships when the worst happens.'

Oakshott nodded. 'How many British subjects are there in Narva?'

Constantinopolous spread his hands and hunched his shoulders. 'Who can tell? No census has ever been taken. You have seen the people who come crowding in to me. If we get twelve hours' notice, we may be able to fill three ships – on the other hand, there will be many in the remote parts of the city and the province who will be left behind.'

'And what will happen to them?'

'The long march to Siberia, perhaps.'

*

When Oakshott left the consul-general's office there was a scuffle amongst the waiting people outside his door to determine who should be the next to see the consul-general. With a sad shake of his head *Javelin*'s captain left the building and continued on up a flight of steps leading from the quay in the opposite direction from where his ship was lying.

A pleasant promenade lay atop the steps. Set with a stand of stately poplars and lined with flowering shrubs, it was a favourite place for the folk of the city to take their evening stroll in the summer months.

Oakshott went on through an archway that led into a public park. Away in the clear light, in the distance, some children were playing ball: their shrill cries came to him across the broad stretch of well-tended grass. He sat on a stone bench, looked at his watch, and addressed himself to contemplating the tree-lined carriageway that bisected the park – and this with the air of a man who waits in expectation.

He had not long to wait. His pulse quickened as something came in sight over the crest of a hill at the far end of the drive. This resolved itself into a pair of horses, and a coachman perched behind. As it drew closer, Oakshott was able to see that the man wore a livery of brown and silver, and behind his back one could discern a coloured parasol, a lady's parasol.

Oakshott rose to his feet when the carriage slowed down. He stepped forward when it came abreast of him, and took off his hat in salute to the vision who sat regarding him with a half-smile that dimpled her right cheek.

'Charles, I am sorry to be late,' she said.

'Only by a couple of minutes, Katerina.'

'If you were truly gallant, you would say that it had seemed an age,' she said.

'It has seemed an age.'

He climbed into the coach and sat beside her. Katerina Jacobson gave an order to her coachman and they turned to go back the way she had come.

'Home for a lovely English tea,' she murmured.

He would have made a suitable response, but her ready lips silenced the words at birth.

The captain's afternoon runs-ashore did not pass unnoticed by *Javelin*'s crew, and gave rise to some speculation not unmixed with hilarity. However, since, upon his return every evening, he called together the officers and senior warrant officers and gave them an account of his meetings with the consul-general, together with the latest news from that source, the ribald speculations were never taken very seriously.

Apart from what might charitably be called Oakshott's secondary interest ashore, he was becoming increasingly concerned that Constantinopolous's reading of the Baltic situation was accurate in every regard, and hourly expected to hear from the consul-general that they were to prepare to sail.

The blow, when it fell, came literally out of the blue.

It happened just after six bells of the forenoon watch. Lieutenant Shacklock was officer of the day and little Cobbold - now fully recovered from his wound - was his midshipman. It was the latter who drew everyone's attention to a large, high-sided merchantman approaching from across the inland lake and shaping course as if to come along *Javelin*'s outboard side. Upon closer inspection, the newcomer was seen to be wearing the Dutch flag.

She was well handled. She came within heaving-line length of the frigate, and someone hailed down from her upper deck:

'Ahoy, English! Will you be taking my lines, please? Only

want to lay alongside you to take on some light stores.'

'Very good!' shouted Shacklock. And to Cobbold: 'See to it, and look lively, Snotty. If you want me, I shall be down with the captain.' And he went below, just as the heaving lines were going across.

It happened that Shacklock, who was navigation officer of the frigate, had chanced to get into conversation with a friendly Norwegian skipper over the ship's side and had negotiated with him for the purchase of a set of locally drawn Baltic charts which must certainly be more accurate than anything *Javelin*'s chart chest contained. He and Oakshott were examining the new acquisitions on the table in the stern cabin. Oakshott had inquired as to the doings of the ship coming alongside and dismissed the matter from his mind upon hearing that it was a friendly Dutchman seeking a billet for an hour or so, when the door burst open without so much as a knock, and little Cobbold stood there, hat in hand and wild-eyed with excitement.

'Can't you learn to knock, lad?' snapped Oakshott.

'Why aren't you on deck?' demanded Shacklock in similar tones. 'Can't I leave you alone for one moment without you falling apart at the seams?'

'Su-sir – the Dutchman . . .' began the boy.

'What of the Dutchman, Mr Cobbold?' asked Oakshott in a more kindly manner. 'Speak out, lad.'

'They – they're making fast mu-mighty strongly up there, sir!'

'Of course they are, *you* –' blazed Shacklock, 'there's an offshore wind.'

'Wu-with chains, sir!'

'*Chains?*'

Oakshott and Shacklock looked at each other.

A second later they brushed past young Cobbold, sending him reeling, and raced out on deck – in time to see a stout chain being hauled from the Dutchman's stern, past *Javelin*'s counter, towards a massive ring bolt set into the stonework of the jetty. Moreover, looking for'ard, Oakshott saw, with a shocking sense of deprivation, that a similar chain had already been secured through a ring bolt and its end brought back and made fast at the Dutchman's bows.

'By God, Shacklock!' he cried. 'We're on the way to being imprisoned here! . . .

'Call all hands!'

It was then, looking up to the deck of the merchantman, that the two officers saw a row of alien faces scowling down at them, and all in an unfamiliar uniform. And each with a levelled musket! They scarcely had time to react to this new shock when the Dutch flag fluttered down, and was replaced by the double-headed eagle of Holy Russia.

'Caught!' muttered Oakshott. 'Caught without a chance to fight!'

As the crew appeared on deck, obedient to the call, they too came within the scope of the line of marksmen – who numbered at least a score – and raised their hands in token of surrender.

A gangplank was lowered from the other ship and an elegant naval officer descended to the frigate's quarter-deck. He doffed his plumed hat to Oakshott and introduced himself in English:

'Commander Rokossovsky, Imperial Russian Navy. I regret, sir, that you are my prisoner. When your crew is all assembled on deck, it will be my duty to read out a proclamation from His Imperial Majesty the Tsar.'

Oakshott bowed grim-faced acquiescence, but kept a dignified silence, preferring first to see which way the cat was going to jump – as the saying goes.

The last of the crew – the slow-movers – arrived on deck. Last of all, the cook from his galley, blinking in the sudden sunlight and wiping his hands on his apron. His expression when he saw the levelled muskets up above would have been risible in any other circumstance.

'Is that all, sir?' asked the Russian.

'When I call for all hands, sir,' responded Oakshott, 'all hands appear. There is never any need to count heads.'

The other nodded. 'Then I will commence,' he said, and taking from his coat-tail pocket a folded sheet of paper, he opened it out with some show of ceremony and read aloud:

' "*By the decree of His Imperial Majesty Paul, Tsar of All the Russias, and in view of the intransigent conduct of the country in question, all British vessels will be subject to embargo in Russian ports. To wit, they will be forbidden entrance to the said ports, and those already berthed in the said ports will not be permitted to leave.*"

'Long live His Imperial Majesty the Tsar!'

There followed the disarming of the ship and crew. The guns were all rendered temporarily useless by the traditional means of driving lead spikes into the touch holes, the powder magazine was double padlocked, likewise the small-arms locker. And – the crowning ignominy – the officers, Oakshott included, were relieved of their swords. A party of Russian marines (the same who had taken part in the stratagem to seize *Javelin* without warning and without a fight) was put aboard to act as custodians of ship and crew: a polite euphemism for jailors.

There was no midday meal served aboard the ship and no one felt hungry enough to demand it; the hands all sat around the upper deck in disconsolate groups. Was it for this that they had given two Frog frigates a bloody nose – to be overpowered by an underhand trick, and not a pistol fired, nor a cutlass swung? This was the burden of their bitter lament.

The officers were grouped in the stern cabin, witnesses to a sad occurrence. The exceedingly civil Commander Rokossovsky had played the devilish trump card of informing Oakshott that he must leave his ship and be escorted to 'some other place'. He had been given an hour to pack enough gear to see him through.

They took wine together, Oakshott and his brothers in arms, while Bantock packed his captain's sea chest with such things as he deemed to be most useful: outer clothing for both summer and winter, small-clothes, writing materials, books, razor and toilet gear, a bottle of brandy, knife, fork, spoon, mug . . .

'Gentlemen, to our next meeting,' said Oakshott. 'Be not put down. All things pass.'

They pledged him, every one. Little Cobbold was crying openly, and the stern and unbending Shacklock looked away when he found to his chagrin that his eyes were prickling.

Oakshott took Brewster to one side. 'Tom, you are now in command,' he said. 'I charge you to guard the interests of all hands and the ship. What will follow, there's no telling. If the tsar joins with Bonaparte and declares war on us, the case will be altered, meanwhile you are merely under embargo. As a ship of war, though unarmed, they'll keep you under close watch and ward. If it comes to war – well, they may deprive you of your ship, but I hope never to see *Javelin* flying enemy colours. Good luck, Tom.'

'And you, sir,' said the former colonial, taking the other's proffered hand. 'Be assured that, while ever I eat King George's victuals and draw his pay, he'll never look to me in vain for loyalty.'

It was a sad parting as Oakshott went over the side, and the whole crew watched in silence – till the shrill voice of a humble powder monkey piped up from a high yardarm:

'Do us all give three cheers for Cap'n Oakshott, what never did a mean thing to any hand aboard this ship!'

Oakshott acknowledged their cheers; then, squaring his shoulders, he strode towards a waiting coach, and two of his sailors followed after, carrying his sea chest.

*

They took him to a fortress called Hermann, which had been built by the Danes in the thirteenth century on the west bank of the River Narva.

His coach and escort were met at the outer end of a drawbridge by a party of soldiers commanded by a young officer, who bade him alight. As he did so, Oakshott saw that a small crowd was gathered at the far end of the square at a respectful distance from the entrance to the fortress, and they were all staring at him. There was a carriage near the crowd, and its driver wore a livery of brown and silver. Oakshott was not able to discern the expression on the face of the woman seated in the carriage because she wore a white face-mask after the Venetian fashion.

As he paused to regard her the woman made a sign to her coachman, upon which he urged his horses forward into a walk. She did not look back as the conveyance trundled out of the square.

'This way, Captain,' murmured the young officer, indicating the drawbridge and the dark maw through the archway.

Beyond the frowning archway was a high-walled courtyard where the sun never came. Oakshott was conducted from it, up a spiral staircase of time-worn stone to a vaulted chamber with narrow, deeply recessed windows that looked out over the quay and the anchorage.

There was a group of men huddled on a long bench at the far end of the chamber. Upon Oakshott's entrance, one of them detached himself and hurried over to greet the newcomer. It was Constantinopolous.

Oakshott scowled at the Greek. 'So much for your twelve-hour warning!' he growled. 'What happened?'

'My agent in Petersburg was arrested two days ago,' said the Greek. He had a livid bruise above his left eye, and had obviously not been taken without a struggle. Oakshott softened towards him.

'I see. And what brought this about?'

'News came through that a combined force of British, Maltese, Portuguese and Neapolitans have forced the French to surrender Malta. It is the end of Tsar Paul's dream. And so . . .' Constantinopolous spread his hands.

Oakshott eyed the group at the end of the chamber. 'And who are those?'

'Some of the more prominent British residents in Narva and the province,' said the other. 'All with their possessions sequestered. Along with myself, they will act as hostages for the good behaviour of the rest of their community. And they are happy to do it, my friend. Anything to save their families from Siberia.'

'Is it war with Russia, then?'

'Not yet, I think. Not if the conduct of the Russian officers is anything to go by. They are most correct.' He touched the contusion over his eye. 'Not so some of their soldiery.'

Further discussion was cut short by a roll of cannonry. Looking out of the window, they saw clouds of white gunsmoke issuing from the ramparts of the castle on the far, eastern side of the river. Oakshott sought out the object of the cannonade, and saw two ships under sail, both moving away from the anchorage and heading downstream.

'That will be a couple of our merchantmen making a break for it,' he murmured. 'May good luck and a fair wind and tide go with them.'

The gunfire continued, but the two sets of white sails never faltered in their passage. Presently the firing slackened and died. Oakshott and the others watched till the last sail vanished from their sight behind a bend in the river.

There came the sound of booted feet coming up the staircase. They turned when the door swung open.

'Captain Oakshott?

'You will come with me, please!'

*

They conducted him to his 'quarters': a large and cleanly swept room in the top floor of one of the ancient towers, furnished sparely with a bed, table, chair, washstand and commode. And his sea chest. Not too bad – as prison cells go, thought Oakshott. There was a narrow arrow-slit of a window which, to his disappointment, looked out over the pine forests of the hinterland and presented not a scrap of blue water. They left him alone and locked the door behind them.

The solitude that the captain of a ship sailing under naval discipline of the noose and the cat o' nine tails must take upon himself for most of his professional life, setting him apart and above those for whom his word is law, is a good schooling for such as monks of an enclosed order, anchorites or prisoners. The slamming and locking of the door struck no terror in Oakshott's breast. When he was alone in his stern cabin and not entertaining his officers, it was to all intents and purposes the self-imposed imprisonment of his rank and station.

He methodically checked the bed and found it to be adequately comfortable and provided with decent clean sheets and blankets. He washed his hands and face, and, seeking a towel in his sea chest, found it to have been searched; everything had been put back carefully enough, but not with Bantock's painstakingness. He rifled through his gear. Nothing seemed to be missing, not even the bottle of brandy. Pouring himself a bumper measure, he took it over to the window and looked out. The bland, wooded landscape offered him no inspiration. He must needs find his own.

What next, Charlie? . . .

Is this to be your lot till all Europe has settled its differences, with George of England, Christian of Denmark, and Paul of Holy Russia gathered to the bosom of

Abraham, and Bonaparte hung from the end of a rope?

Shall you ever tread the decks of *Javelin* again, and feel the sheer delight of a good landfall, a fair wind, the sound of a thrumming sail, the splash of spindrift? . . .

The sun was already touching the edge of the trees on the horizon. So much had happened that day, he had scarcely noticed the passing of time. Odd, when one's whole life was once dictated by the ringing of bells at every half-hour through the day and night, and one was so bound up with every shifting pattern of natural forces, from the state of the sea and sky to the movement of the stars in the heavens, suddenly to have lost track of something so simple and fundamental as the dying of a day.

He took another pull of his brandy.

And then, there was – *she* . . .

What there was – what there had been – between them, was no one's business but their own. That much was sacrosanct and, he was convinced, separate from any other consideration that might, or might not, have led Katerina Jacobson to follow her scoundrelly brother's coat tails and pursue him from Mogg's Diversions to the Christiansborg palace, and from there to draw him to her at the Villa Jacobson.

In short, his male pride was at the test. Was it for his own sake that she had pursued him? Or was she working on behalf of Bernstorff, to suborn a captain of the Royal Navy for his own tortuous ends? Or was there something of both motives?

A sign – even a small gesture of the hand – when their eyes had met across the square below the fortress might have given him a clue. Instead of that – nothing.

A bad day, Charlie. In one fell swoop you lose your freedom, your ship, and a mistress.

And for how long?

NINE

For how long? . . .

Oakshott reiterated this same question throughout the darkness of a sub-arctic winter, one of the worst in living memory.

Accustomed from early youth as a midshipman to interminable months in the grey-blue deserts of the world's oceans with never a foot set on land and only tantalizing glimpses of shore life seen from afar, he found the existence in his high tower considerably less of a burden than it would have been to most others.

The swift end of the summer brought biting cold, but they – the keepers of the fortress – provided him with ample cut wood for the open fireplace in the room. The food was both excellent and plentiful, being largely comprised of fish – fresh, salted, smoked or pickled. They also allowed him beer and wine to his requirement, along with the distilled white spirit of the region. In all – as any deep-sea sailor who had done blockade duty in Biscay, or convoy work in the Atlantic would have attested – it was as soft a winter as could have been hoped for.

But it was a horse of a very different colour from freedom!

Commander Rokossovsky, the officer who had commanded the coup against *Javelin*, became from the first a regular visitor. At least once a week this very civilized Russian would call upon him, always with a gift of some sort – a jar of honey, a bottle of brandy, some books in English;

and he was a mine of – admittedly – limited information in such matters as the wellbeing of *Javelin* and her crew. In answer to whether they were all in good heart, Rokossovsky was able to inform him that the officers had all accepted parole, in consequence of which they were free to move around in the strict limits of the dockyard area. Questioned about the embargo, Rokossovsky was able to tell him that the two British merchantmen who fled the embargo had in fact got clean away, but that the third – which had made no attempt to escape – had been burned.

'*Burned* – you mean – by your people?' asked Oakshott, appalled.

'By order of the tsar,' admitted Rokossovsky, and had the grace to look ashamed. Clearly, there were no limits to the vagaries of Russia's eccentric ruler.

Rokossovsky, questioned about Constantinopolous, was very amusing. It appeared that the Greek – ever a survivor – had been held in custody for only a day.

'In addition to being your country's consul-general in Narva,' explained the Russian, 'Constantinopolous also represents the interests of the principality of Andorra. He successfully pleaded that, though a country which can comfortably be ridden right round in a day, it is closely associated with France. In our present political climate, that was enough to win him his freedom. The flag of Andorra flies over the former British consulate and it is business as usual.'

Oakshott touched only once upon the subject of Katerina Jacobson who, as he rightly guessed, was well known to the other by name and repute. Rokossovsky was singularly unforthcoming about that enigmatic beauty.

'The baroness has left Narva, that is for certain,' he said, 'but where she has gone, I couldn't say. Petersburg, perhaps? No, her brother the count has not been seen here for over a year. Would you care for a game of chess, my dear fellow?'

Both men played a good game of chess: the Russian

habitually employed a classic tradition of delaying attack till he had completed his development, moving each centre pawn once, each knight and bishop once, getting the queen off the back row, and castling – all the time parrying every threat from his opponent; on his good days, this tactic won him a game after a dozen moves. Oakshott worked on the excellent premise that there is no combination without positional advantage, and that a specific winning sequence of moves cannot be found if there is no superiority on which to base it.

The trouble was that neither of them had any great flexibility of play, and during the long winter evenings each came to know the other's basic game as well as his own, so there were frequent stalemates. Indeed, if their acquaintance had lasted into the spring, they would probably have turned to whist.

But that was not to be.

The end of it all came as suddenly and unexpectedly as the beginning. Oakshott, after an excellent supper of broiled lobster, had employed himself by writing up the diary that he had kept since he first went to sea; next he read a few pages of his favourite Henry Fielding, then washed and prepared himself for bed. He had scarcely knelt to say his prayers when there came a faint tap on the door, followed by the sound of the key turning gently in the lock. The manner in which this was done being in itself unique, if not suspicious, Oakshott took three swift paces across the room and snatched up the pair of sizeable fire tongs from the hearth, hefted them in his hand and – mindful of legends of murdered prisoners – prepared to give a good account of himself before he went down.

The door opened. It was Rokossovsky. He was carrying a small valise. He looked surprised and not unalarmed to see Oakshott standing four-square and ready for anything.

'Put that damned thing down, my dear fellow,' said the Russian.

'What are you doing here at this hour?' demanded the other.

For answer, Rokossovsky up-ended the valise, and a pile of clothing – civilian fustian – tumbled out on to the bed.

'Put these on,' he said. 'Quickly, Oakshott. We have exactly five minutes before the guard changes at midnight.'

Long experience of the hardest occupation known to man had taught Oakshott instant obedience to a firm order given in circumstances that seemed to promise a profitable outcome. He had on a coarse woollen shirt, a pair of grey flannel breeches, and a rough neckcloth tied before he posed the question:

'Where are we going, Rokossovsky?'

'You, my friend, are rejoining your fleet,' responded the other. 'Well, don't stand staring, man. Put on the cloak and hat. Your own boots will suffice – I didn't know how big your feet were.'

It was as silent as the tomb in the great fortress. And as dark as Old Nick's pocket. With Rokossovsky leading, the two men descended the narrow spiral staircase that led from the top of the tower. Oakshott, his mind in some confusion following the Russian's astonishing declaration about his proposed destination, addressed himself to concentrating upon the immediate task in hand. His thoughts were sharpened to a point when, upon reaching the bottom, Rokossovsky clutched at his arm and whispered for silence. As they listened, from far off down a long barrel-vaulted stone corridor that led to some remote fastness of the fortress, came the sound of marching boots.

'The new guard!' breathed Rokossovsky. 'Our time is running out fast! Come!'

The great door of the fortress was open to the night –

presumably by Rokossovsky's agency, thought Oakshott – and they stepped out into the snow-covered courtyard. More snow was coming down, swirling around the dark vault contained by the four towering, black walls.

A sentry with a bayoneted musket stood guard on the massive gate to the drawbridge. He came to the ready, point advanced, and hissed a challenge as the two men approached him.

Rokossovsky responded in their language, and the soldier lowered his weapon. Close enough, now, to see his face, Oakshott discerned him to be both young and frightened. Rokossovsky must also have sensed the other's fear, for he laid a reassuring hand on the youth's shoulder – and won for himself a faint, brave smile.

Propping his musket against the wall, the sentry unbolted and swung open the gate. Ahead, Oakshott could see the snow-covered drawbridge and the square beyond. In the middle of the square stood a substantial four-horse travelling coach.

'Take it, Oakshott,' said Rokossovsky, pointing. 'This is where we part. And may good fortune go with you.'

Oakshott sought, and held, his proffered hand.

'I don't understand . . .' he began.

'All will be explained to you,' said the Russian. 'Go, now – the guard will be here at any moment.'

'Of course,' said Oakshott, well aware that his sometime chess opponent must be taking an appalling risk to be doing what he was – not forgetting the young sentry, nor – now that his eyes had become accustomed to the darkness set off against the glare of the snow – at least two other soldiers who were stationed about the courtyard and affecting to notice nothing of what was going on.

A last squeeze of hand, and Oakshott plunged through the gate, which was immediately slammed and bolted behind him. Running pell-mell through the ankle-deep snow, he came at length to the waiting coach. The driver was already opening the door for him to mount; the fellow's hat was pulled low over his brow and his high-collared, caped coat hid the rest of his face.

It was surprisingly warm in the coach interior, and a heady scent hung upon the air. A shadowy figure was seated in the opposite corner. The scent – so well remembered – and a sixth sense of presence, told Oakshott all he needed to know.

'Katerina!' he murmured.

'I thought you were never coming, Charles,' whispered she.

Stooping, he embraced her. Retaining his hand, she pulled him down to sit beside her, and spread a half of her fur rug over his knees. Almost immediately after, the coach gave a lurch and moved off, jouncing on its springs over the packed snow.

'Where are we bound for?' asked Oakshott.

'For Riga.'

'Riga I have heard of. A Baltic port somewhat south of here.'

'Some two hundred miles south of here – as the crow flies.'

'Aaaah.'

'And ice-free.'

'Ice-free – aaah!'

'There are posting houses along the way,' she said. 'And we have ample victuals here in the coach.'

'You are accompanying me, Katerina?'

'Only as far as Riga.'

'And – at Riga?'

'There will be a ship awaiting to take you to your destination.'

'I see.' He relaxed in the comfortable seat, enjoying the cosseting warmth, the nearness of her. 'This enterprise was uncommonly well arranged, Katerina, but I confess myself puzzled as to Rokossovsky's part in it. Not in yours, I hasten to add: nothing you do will ever puzzle or surprise me again.'

She laughed. 'Well then, I should explain that Rokossovsky is more Estonian than Russian,' she said. 'And the Estonians will never accept Russian rule, with or without the oppression that goes with it.'

'And the soldiers on guard duty when I escaped?'

'They would have been more of Rokossovsky's kind,' she said, with a distinct note of disinterest. 'My dear, one has to learn to use these people by taking advantage of their various allegiances.'

'That sounds very cynical, Katerina,' he said. 'Such a remark puts me in mind of your brother and his philosophy.'

'I am the sister of my brother!' she snapped. 'In some ways – in many ways – we are indivisible.'

This small exchange imposed a slight restraint upon them and they were silent for a while. Oakshott made a chink in the window curtains and looked out. They seemed to have come to the outskirts of the town. A dark farmstead with a long low barn loomed up and slipped past into the night. They were now travelling over an unmade road that was deeply rutted under the packed snow. He sat back in his seat and relaxed again.

'And what is the purpose of all this?' he asked. 'This charade. I am taken away from my ship and imprisoned. Most comfortably, I might add. The food – excellent. The company – well, Rokossovsky plays a very tolerable game of chess. I've done longer spells at sea in more discomfort and worse company. What now?'

'Your imprisonment was by order of the tsar,' she said, 'whose embargo included a footnote that all captains of Royal Navy ships were to be closely detained. It is Paul's intent, you see, that if it comes to war with England, he will have the likes of *Javelin* to add to his fleet. He would not want such captains as the gallant Lord Charles Oakshott to contrive a daring escape down the River Narva with all guns blazing.'

'I am flattered by the tsar's attention,' said Oakshott. 'But why, exactly, have you contrived my escape? Always supposing that you did not do it for tender motives of regard for me.'

She ignored his gentle imputation. 'Your escape was contrived by my brother,' she said, 'in concert with Rokossovsky and the other Estonian patriots. Happily, the tsar's order for your imprisonment prevented you from having to give your parole, like your officers. Knowing your strong sense of honour, my brother knew that, once given, your parole would render you useless for the role that he has written for you.'

'And what role is that?'

'Axel has recently returned from Paris where he has ostensibly been working to bring about the *rapprochement* that the tsar seeks with Bonaparte. He has returned with copies of letters that Paul and Bonaparte have exchanged – letters of such a sensational nature that they must be communicated to the British Prime Minister immediately. Your role, my dear Charles, is to convey my brother's dispatch to the commander-in-chief of the British fleet which is at present lying off Copenhagen, and request that he sends it on to London in his swiftest ship.'

Katerina was tireless. As their coach rolled on through the night she continued to ply him with facts with which Bernstorff had supplied her, and to answer all – or most of – his questions.

'This fleet you speak of, Katerina,' said Oakshott. 'Are you referring to the squadron that Admiral Dixon took to Copenhagen last summer, when you and I met for the second time?'

'No,' she replied. 'The fleet of which I speak is assembling for the purpose of attacking – and taking – Copenhagen!'

'Is it, by heaven!' he exclaimed. 'And how do you – I should say, how does your brother – come to know of this?'

'Axel advised the move,' was her reply. 'You see, in imitation of the tsar, the Danish king has now put a similar embargo on British ships, in addition to which, Danish troops have occupied Lübeck with a view to wrecking British trade there. Axel foresaw both moves last September and advised Pitt that it would be necessary for him to knock Denmark out of the conflict by destroying her navy and taking Copenhagen.'

Oakshott shook his head in wonderment at the labyrinth of European politics in which his companion's brother appeared to move with such assurance and masterful authority.

'And it was upon this advice that a fleet was gathered?' he asked. 'Who, then, is commanding it?'

'Admiral Sir Hyde Parker.'

'Hyde Parker?' repeated Oakshott in tones of vast disbelief. 'Hyde *Parker*? But he is a burnt-out hulk. Never was a great leader at his best, and totally incapable of carrying out the commission of assaulting a stronghold like Copenhagen. Pitt must have taken leave of his senses to have allowed the Admiralty such an appointment.'

'And as Hyde Parker's second in command,' said Katerina. 'He has – Nelson.'

'Nelson! Aaaah! That's more like it. Nelson could do it,' said Oakshott. 'Indeed, I don't know of another admiral in the navy who could crack a tough nut like Copenhagen.' His voice took on a note of fond reminiscence. 'I saw him envelop the French at the Nile, you know. I was there, watching from the shore. I saw him accomplish a victory of total annihilation, the like of which has not been equalled in the annals of warfare since Cannae. By heaven, if Nelson is to lead the van, I would give anything to sail with him!'

'Very commendable of you, Charles,' drawled his companion. 'And now, we have talked this matter through and it is past two o'clock. It's hardly likely that we shall reach Riga much before midnight tomorrow and it will be a tiring journey. I would suggest that we have some sleep while we are able. Would you first like a nightcap? Brandy?'

'Most assuredly, madame.'

By the light of the single lantern that illuminated the interior of the coach (which was also furnished with a wood-burning stove for heating purposes), Katerina Jacobson produced from a hanging cupboard a flask of brandy and two goblets. Oakshott did the honours, pouring them each a stiff bumper.

They touched glasses, and their eyes met.

'To eventual victory,' she murmured.

'Your brother once pledged me with a similar toast,' said Oakshott, 'and I give you the same response – whose victory?'

'Ours,' she said.

'Damn me, if that wasn't his reply also!' cried Oakshott. 'And a good toast it makes, too!'

They touched glasses and drank deeply.

The coach rolled on its way, across the wrinkled plain of Estonia, past darkened villages and gaunt manor houses under the snow, rattling on at a steady trot, stopping for nothing and no one. Inside, the wood stove burned low and neither occupant felt the need to replenish it as, tumbled together under the warm fur rug, they pursued arcane delights which were entirely their own business.

Later – much later – Oakshott was aroused from a pleasant torpor by the sound of his silver goblet, lately discarded, rolling back and forth across the floor of the coach. A most irritating noise it made, too. But he did not feel inclined to arouse his companion, who was asleep and sweetly scented, her head resting on his bare shoulder.

A man may bear worse hardships.

It was bitingly cold on the quayside at Riga. A screaming dawn, with a bell buoy clanging somewhere out in the murk. The boat from the fast cutter which was to take him to Copenhagen roads and join Hyde Parker's fleet was rolling in the shallows at a discreet distance, waiting to be called in. The coxswain and oarsmen peered up at the two figures standing on the quay and speculated, each after his own fashion.

'We shall meet again, Katerina,' said Oakshott.

'It is possible,' she murmured. 'But on the whole unlikely.'

'Why so?' he demanded.

For answer, she first laid a gentle finger across his lips.

'No more questions,' she said. 'They have all been asked, and answered. Leave it be at that, Charles. I may not see you again, but I shall communicate with you – and that very soon. Be content till you have heard from me. And then you will understand all.'

The Estonian seamen, huddled on their thwarts and blowing on their frozen fingers, watched in mounting irritation at what seemed to them to be an unconscionably protracted dalliance on the part of the tall man and the – even at that distance – discernibly beautiful woman; but presently their agonies were over; the tall man detached himself from the woman and waved to the coxswain. They plied their oars and took the boat alongside.

Charles Oakshott stood in the stern sheets as the oarsmen gave way and the boat shaped course out into the middle of the harbour, in the direction of the bell buoy that struck to his ear like the tolling for the Dead.

He watched the woman on the quay till the icy mists closed in between them. Just before she was shut out of his sight, and he from hers, she raised a hand in a final gesture of farewell.

Part Four

TO BATTLE!

TEN

Off Elsinore, Denmark
30 March 1801

Dearest Mine,

The weather having greatly improved, I today had myself rowed round the fleet, which is looking very fine, so that I am emboldened to think that our present enterprise may be successful after all, that is if I am able to prevail upon Ld Nelson to restrain himself from one of his more audacious proposals to date. I will not tire yr pretty head with details, dearest mine, but it is certain that I shall have to be more than firm with his Ldship, or we shall be faced with an ignominious defeat, for as I continue to remind him, this is not the eastern Mediterranean, nor Copenhagen the barren shore of Abu Quir. Oh, what have I done to deserve such a commission and at a time in my career when I might have expected to spend my last days in the king's service more tranquilly employd?

I wd not have you think there is any difference twixt Nelson and me. He is such a sweet-natured fellow that every heart leans toward him. Imagine, last week he did send over to me the present of a fresh caught turbut which served me well for supper and three guests and all.

Dearest mine, I am so missing you . . .

Admiral Sir Hyde Parker, commander in chief of the British fleet lying off Copenhagen roads, and carrying his flag in the three-decker HMS *London*, sat back in his chair, sucked on the end of his pen and contemplated the letter that he was composing for his young wife, the new delight of his advancing age: she who, forty-four years his junior and prettily buxom, was referred to by his officers – behind their hands – as 'Batter Pudding'.

Difficult to express, even to one so warm-hearted as his Dearest, that he bore no malice towards Nelson. It was just that – well – he was one of the newer fellows, given to the new tactics that ill-accorded with one's training, one's standards. The way in which Nelson had cut out of the line at St Vincent, for instance. Brilliant move, as it turned out, but anyone but that fellow with his confounded luck would have been court martialled and disgraced. Nelson and his luck. Take the Nile – a flash in the pan if there ever was one.

And now he's contemplating another stroke of luck here in Copenhagen. Well, one supposes one must give the fellow his head – up to a point. But he will have to be watched.

With a sigh, Hyde Parker addressed himself to his letter, the latter part of which, being largely concerned with endearments to the charming little thing who still retained for him all the unexpected delights of a new toy, was not difficult to compose.

There came a tap on the cabin door just as the admiral was sanding the letter.

'Come in. Aaah, it's you, Gervase,' – his flag lieutenant.

'Admiral, there's a new arrival on board – Captain Lord Charles Oakshott of *Javelin*. I think he's known to you, sir.'

'Oakshott? Yes, I know him of old. Isn't he the? . . . and wasn't *Javelin* the? . . .'

'Embargoed in Narva, sir. That's right.'

'Well, how did he get back here?'

'Lord Charles didn't say, sir.'

'Well, show him in, Gervase, show him in!'

'Aye, aye, sir.'

The flag lieutenant departed and presently returned with Oakshott, still in his civilian fustian, with a boat cloak and a villainous looking tall hat that he had acquired from somewhere.

'Aaah, Oakshott.'

'Admiral.'

Hyde Parker's amiable glance fell upon his visitor with approval. He pointed to the other and nodded. 'I remember you well, Oakshott,' he said. '*Spartiate*, was it not?'

'That's right, Sir Hyde. I did two commissions in *Spartiate*, one as mid, one as third lieutenant under your command.'

'Be seated, my dear fellow, and tell me what you're about. And why all – *this* . . .' With an expressive gesture, the C-in-C encompassed Oakshott's fustian, his somewhat bedraggled appearance, unshaven jowls the tall hat.

Flag Lieutenant Gervase poured sherry, and Oakshott gave the admiral a brief résumé of his doings since *Javelin* had arrived in Narva the previous autumn, to which Hyde Parker listened intently without interrupting.

'And your voyage from Riga,' he said, when Oakshott had finished, 'this was effected by these – Estonian patriots, as you describe them?'

'The fast schooner was skippered and manned by excellent fellows, sir,' replied the other, 'who would have faced worse than imprisonment, I fancy, if they had been caught transporting an escaped prisoner of the tsar.'

'Greatly to their credit,' declared the admiral. 'Much to their honour, I'm sure. And this dispatch – these matters of a sensational nature which must be delivered to the Prime Minister without delay . . .'

'The Baroness Jacobson was most insistent, sir,' said Oakshott. 'Mr Pitt must see that material with all dispatch.'

'Not Mr Pitt, sir,' drawled Gervase. 'During your absence, Mr Pitt resigned in favour of Mr Addington.'

'Addington, that's right, ha-ha!' guffawed the admiral. 'And not very highly regarded is our Mr Addington.' He beamed up at his aide. 'What was that mighty amusing quip that was going the rounds when we left England, Gervase? Touching upon the disparity betwixt Pitt and Addington. What was it, hey?'

Gervase preened himself: he was clearly a man who enjoyed holding the floor with a good anecdote.

'It was put about,' said he, 'that, as Pitt is a city, so Addington is merely a borough. And the thought was encapsulated in a verse which expresses it thuswise:

'Pitt is to Addington
As London is to Paddington.'

'Capital, capital!' Hyde Parker slapped his ample thigh. 'What d'you think of that, hey, Oakshott?'

'Most risible, sir,' responded Oakshott. 'As regards the dispatch, it is addressed to you, so one must assume that there is a commentary contained within it to yourself, as well as the material for the eyes of the Prime Minister.'

'Let us see it then, Oakshott. Produce it,' boomed the admiral.

From the breast pocket of his fustian coat Oakshott took out a packet wrapped in oiled silk. The missive was clearly addressed on the outside to Sir Hyde Parker.

'Open it, Gervase,' ordered the admiral.

The flag lieutenant did so. 'Sir, there is a note to yourself,' he said, 'and another sealed packet addressed to the Prime Minister.'

'Read the communication addressed to me, Gervase,' said his master, 'for your young eyes are better than mine.'

Gervase broke the seal on the note in question, and read aloud from the contents:

' "From His Britannic Majesty's Consul-General in Narva, addressed to Admiral Sir Hyde Parker, KCB *. . ." '*

'Well, I'm glad to hear that Constantinopolous is still representing our interests,' interjected Oakshott. 'And none better.'

'Indeed, indeed?' said Hyde Parker. 'Continue, Gervase.'

'"*The contents of the attached report, gathered by Count Axel Bernstorff and brought to my attention by his sister the Baroness Jacobson, may well prove to be the vital key to the present intrigues being carried out between the tsar and Bonaparte, and I cannot express too forcibly my conviction that the report should be brought to the Prime Minister's attention with the utmost haste. Signed,* C.C. *Constantinopolous, HM Consul-General, Narva.*"'

'Well that minces no matters,' said Hyde Parker. 'Gervase, do you have the report dispatched at once. What fast ships have we that can be spared without much loss of firepower?'

Gervase was more than a good recounter of anecdotes; like a born flag lieutenant, he had the answer at his fingertips:

'There is the cutter *Joris*, sir,' he said. 'And *Argo*, *Silenus*, and *Pickle*, schooners. I would advise *Argo*, sir.'

'*Argo* it shall be, Gervase,' said the admiral. 'See to it right away. Have her set sail forthwith.'

'Aye, aye, sir.' The flag lieutenant was about to depart with the packet when a folded slip of paper fell from it and fluttered to the deck; he stooped to pick it up.

'Aah, I missed this,' he said. 'It's another note that was tucked inside the packet - and addressed to you, Lord Charles.'

Oakshott took the missive. It felt very small. Insubstantial. His name was inscribed upon the face in warm, sloping and unmistakably feminine handwriting, and he knew upon the instant who had penned it there.

'Thank you,' he said. And slipped it into his pocket.

'Well, now, Oakshott,' said Hyde Parker, when Gervase had gone. 'What's to be done with you, hey?'

(From Katerina, he thought. Is this, then, the communication of which she spoke - the one that would come very soon? Soon enough - I have carried it with me from Riga!)

'I should like, if possible, to be given employment in the coming enterprise, Admiral,' he said. 'In any capacity whatever, it goes without saying.'

'Well, there is no command for you, Oakshott, I regret,' said the other. 'My best thought is that you attend upon Lord Nelson aboard his flagship *St George*. Address yourself to him and ask him how you may be of service in his assault squadron, which is like to close with the Copenhagen defences within the next few days.'

'Thank you, I will do that, sir,' said Oakshott, rising.

'Another sherry?'

'Thank you, no, sir.'

(Straight to report to Nelson – but, first, to read her communication . . .)

The admiral rose and gave Oakshott his hand.

'I wish you well in this coming enterprise, Oakshott,' he said. 'You did splendidly to escape from the damned Russkies, and I greatly commiserate with you for the loss of *Javelin*. But then, we may yet see her safe return. Good luck to you – I am sure that Lord Nelson will make full use of your talents.

'We – that is to say, I – have great hopes for Lord Nelson and his plans to destroy the Danish fleet and take Copenhagen,' he concluded. 'Yes – great hopes.'

So saying, he cast a wistful glance to the miniature of the eighteen-year-old child bride that stood upon his desk. And sighed.

The busy gangway of a fleet flagship in the throes of a coming engagement is no place for an unprepossessingly unshaven individual to be requesting a boat to take him away. The officer of the day simply turned his back on Oakshott and shouted orders to an ammunition lighter that was coming alongside. The duty quartermaster fobbed him off on his deputy – who had absented himself on some other business. The midshipman of the day simply ignored him and went on reading flag signals through his telescope.

In the end, he was rescued by Gervase. This energetic officer, having carried out his task of sending the schooner *Argo* to England with the Bernstorff report, smartly brought the officer of the day's attention to the importance of the tall man in fustian. A boat was called away, and within five minutes Oakshott was going over the side with full captain's honours piped after him.

There was a steep swell in the fleet anchorage. As his boat progressed through the long lines of high-sided battleships, Oakshott was obliged to hold on to his thwart with one hand whilst he groped in his pocket and brought out the letter to read . . .

All about him the sons of Albion were preparing for battle. On the fo'c's'les of two- and three-deck ships of the line, red-coated marines drilled and counter-marched; batteries of long cannon were run in and run out to order; topmen swarmed in the yards, taking sail in and out to the cries of their petty officers; bugles blared and kettle drums beat out their staccato rhythms. The fleet was at exercise for war – its only reason for being.

Oblivious to all this, Charles Oakshott sat and read the letter from a woman who – though he scarcely admitted it to himself – had played a small havoc with his life and his emotions. Indeed, he had time to read it through half a dozen times slowly, for the letter, though memorable as to content, was brief as could be.

For the rest of the journey through the fleet, he simply sat and stared out across the blue-grey waters.

'*St George* ahoy!' The coxswain's hail woke him from his reverie.

'What ship?' From Nelson's flagship.

'*London*! With a ship's captain to come aboard you!'

'Ship's captain – aye, aye!'

They did him the honours over the side, and not by so

much as a sly grin did the gangway staff express their thoughts on the oddly dressed ship's captain as he set foot upon their hallowed quarter-deck and raised his tall hat in salute.

'Well, by all that's holy – *Charlie Oakshott!*'

Oakshott, in the act of making his wants known to the officer of the day, turned at the sound of a voice that carried overtones of a long-forgotten familiarity, and met the smiling gaze of a man about his own age – red-headed, freckled, inclining to stoutness. It took a few moments to place him as a former messmate.

'Toby Catlin, as ever was!' he exclaimed. 'Well, how are you, old fellow?'

Catlin and he had been midshipmen together, and had both shown equal promise of advancement. The wayward fate that directs the advancement of men, however, was disconcertingly apparent from the fact that Catlin was still a mere lieutenant. Indeed, as they spoke, his companion, metaphorically stripping away Charles Oakshott's fustian and discerning the habiliments of a ship's captain underneath, markedly amended his manner of address.

'Then what brings you aboard *St George* – um – sir?' he asked; but still smiling, still the happy-go-lucky Toby Catlin with whom Oakshott had enjoyed so many riotous runs ashore from Portsmouth to Tobago.

Oakshott told him, and went on: 'Toby, can you lend me some gear? Some small-clothes and an old undress coat will serve.'

'By all means. Come on down to the wardroom. As to seeing the admiral – he is going to address a meeting of the captains and other officers of the assault squadron at eight bells. I see no reason why you shouldn't insinuate yourself into that distinguished gathering – sir. Have you met his lordship?'

'Twice, Toby. Whether he'll remember me's another question.'

St George's wardroom was aft on the middle deck and comprised the usual quite spacious dining quarters with a row of cubicled cabins leading off. Catlin's cubbyhole barely contained the two of them, his gear and all, as the good-natured fellow opened up his sea chest and produced Oakshott's wants. The breeches were a little slack around the crotch, and the coat fitted not too well at the neck, but the get-up was a vast improvement on the fustian.

'It wants twenty minutes to eight bells,' said Toby Catlin, consulting his watch. 'Will you join me in a dram – sir?'

'By all means, Toby,' said Oakshott. 'And many thanks.'

Before Oakshott and his old shipmate had half finished their drink and relived several long-gone runs ashore, boats were crowding at *St George*'s gangway and disgorging senior officers from Nelson's squadron. When eight bells rang out, Catlin escorted Oakshott to the admiral's day cabin which lay aft on the upper deck. A queue of officers was dribbling in past a pair of marine sentries and a fussy civilian secretary who was making some attempt to tally their names and stations with a list he had. Toby Catlin cut through this functionary's hesitant doubts about the lieutenant in the ill-fitting undress coat:

'Captain Lord Charles Oakshott of *Javelin*!' he snapped.

The former shipmates shook hands.

'Good luck, Charlie. I hope we may toast each other again after the battle.'

'I shall greatly look forward to that, Toby.'

The day cabin was a charivari of voices and unbearably stuffy from the concert of forty or so men who were packed in there. With the advantage of his superior height Oakshott was able to peer over their heads from the back row and sight the slight figure seated at the table with his back to the stern windows. Nelson was talking to a civilian clerk at his elbow.

Three years had passed since his last encounter with the victor of the Nile battle, and Oakshott was unprepared for the change which the pressure of great events had wrought upon the little admiral.

He was in undress, with replicas of two stars embroidered upon the left breast and the Nile medal at his throat. The lean face was drawn and pale, and there was a green shade over the left eye. The hand that gesticulated in his address to the listening clerk was fine-boned, delicate, sensitive. But it was only when one regarded his right – good – eye and considered the quirky mobility of his full and expressive lips, and took in the wiry energy contained in his slender frame that one became aware of the daemonic force that drove Horatio Nelson.

His peroration with the clerk completed, the admiral had only to look up and regard the gathering for the chattering to cease the way the cawing of rooks in high trees is silenced when a hawk passes overhead.

'Will someone please open a window,' said the victor of the Nile. 'It's quite unbearably stuffy in here. Thank you, Fremantle.'

The admiral rose to his feet. 'Gentlemen, I will not take up too much of your valuable time,' he said. 'My object today is, firstly to inform you of my general intent in the coming battle, and then to proceed to my plan of attack.

'As regards my theory of strategy, those captains among you who served with me at the Nile – I speak of Captain Foley of *Elephant* and Captain Thompson of *Bellona* – will know that in my opinion the boldest methods are the safest, and that a vigorous exertion of our force, directed with judgement, will best serve our country's cause. So much for strategy.'

The admiral then made a sign with his hand, contingent upon which a couple of midshipmen brought in a blackboard upon which was limned in chalk a chart of Copenhagen roads and environs, showing in particular the elongated patch of shallows surrounded by deep water that immediately faced the city and harbour.

'The Danish fleet, as you know, gentlemen, is moored in one straight line of nineteen battleships on the edge of the shallows fronting the city. In a sense, we have a tactical situation similar to that which we faced at the Nile. However, there is the vital difference: the Danes are moored fore and aft and there is not room for even a bum-boat to get inshore of them – as Captain Foley' – and here Nelson's blue-grey eye lit upon his old comrade – 'as Captain Foley's *Goliath* did at the Nile.

'My intent therefore, gentlemen, and I have the agreement of Sir Hyde on this issue, is to take our assault squadron right round the Middle Ground shallows – so' – and he described a clockwise circle with his forefinger – 'and engage the Danish fleet where they least expect us – from the south. Meanwhile, Sir Hyde and the remainder of the fleet will be in the north to give us such support as may be needed, particularly with regard to the Trekroner batteries.

'Any questions so far?'

There were no questions. Nelson's intent was all perfectly clear. He continued to enlarge upon it.

Oakshott listened to the speaker, enrapt, even the letter that was burning a hole in his coat-tail pocket forgotten. The little admiral's exposition was so clear, concise, bearing upon the mind with the inevitability of the obvious, that his listeners were charmed out of all thought of disagreement with his propositions.

This, and only this, was the way to destroy the Danish fleet by a *coup de main* and take Copenhagen!

When Nelson had finished he sat down, and his servant brought him a glass of white wine. The little admiral, quite visibly aware that he had had a tremendous effect upon the gathering, and unselfconsciously glad of it, listened to the earnest plaudits of his subordinates, whilst not permitting the slightest hint of flattery or sycophancy; a captain who shall be nameless essayed such a tack and was rewarded with silence and a blank stare.

Oakshott stayed at the rear of the crowd surrounding the table where Nelson sat, patiently awaiting his turn to address the admiral. His height, however, betrayed him. Looking up, Nelson espied the man with the parti-coloured eyes.

'As I live and breathe – Oakshott!' he exclaimed.

'My lord.' Oakshott stepped forward and took the admiral's proffered hand.

'Gentlemen,' said Nelson, addressing those nearest to them, 'may I present Captain Lord Charles Oakshott, who is a man of many parts. He served with me at the Nile, but it is not generally known that his place in that battle was actually aboard the French flagship, where, I am sure, he was a veritable cuckoo in the nest and wrought considerable damage.'

Oakshott was immediately the centre of interest, and found himself shaking hands with the captains who would be in the forefront of the coming battle: Walker of *Isis*, Fremantle of *Ganges*, Lawford of *Polyphemus*, Foley of *Elephant* . . .

'I was apprised of *Javelin*'s fate, Oakshott,' said Nelson. 'But how is it that you are here? Were you perhaps paroled?'

Oakshott gave the admiral a brief account of his escape, and also touched upon his reason for coming aboard the flagship.

'Indeed, you shall find employment in our coming venture, my dear fellow,' said Nelson. 'There'll be no command for you, more's the pity, but I am sure you will not object to serving under another.' He turned to the clerk. 'Joplin, do we know of any captain who is short of a first lieutenant or the like?'

The clerk thought for a moment. 'Ah, but I do believe

that *Glatton*'s gunnery officer fell ill and had to be returned to England by dispatch boat yesterday, Admiral. Undoubtedly Captain Bligh would be most grateful for such a replacement . . .'

'Capital notion – capital!' cried Nelson. 'Bligh – Bligh, where are you? Come forward, I have good news for you.'

'My lord?' The speaker who came forward was a well-set-up and pleasant-featured man in his late forties. Oakshott had never made his acquaintance, but everyone in the navy knew him by name and reputation as 'Bligh of the *Bounty*', after the exploit which had brought him a certain mixed fame.

'Bligh, this is Oakshott of *Javelin*, who is volunteering for service in the coming battle. Will you engage him as your temporary gunnery officer?'

Bligh's hazel-coloured eyes flickered over Oakshott searchingly, and the latter felt a touch of unease beneath the scrutiny. However, the other seemed to approve of what he saw. He extended his hand.

'Be delighted to have you aboard, Oakshott,' said the captain of *Glatton*.

The meeting over, Oakshott joined his new commanding officer in his cutter and was rowed over to *Glatton*.

'So *Javelin* is still restrained by the Russians, eh?' asked Bligh.

'She is,' replied Oakshott. 'Nor have I seen her since the day I was taken off and locked away.'

'I sympathize with you,' said the other, and a shadow seemed to pass over his finely chiselled countenance. 'It is a great and terrible blow to a captain – to lose his ship.' And he looked away across the water.

Sensing the note of awkwardness, and divining the reason, Oakshott changed the subject.

'*Glatton*, I remember from Channel patrols,' he said, 'and

at the blockading of Brest in 'ninety-seven. A fifty-six-gunner, is she not?'

Bligh nodded. 'That is so, but we have experimented by replacing the six for'ard twelve-pounders, port and starboard, with carronades, so that, together with the usual pair on the fo'c's'le, she carries an uncommonly fine broadside at close range.'

'Indeed she does,' said Oakshott, and made a swift calculation. 'A broadside of seven sixty-eight-pound balls – that's nearly half a ton of iron in the air at once!'

Bligh grinned, and one saw in a trice that there was a lively sense of humour behind his rather stiff manner. 'Enough to give the Danes second thoughts about putting the embargo on our ships, I fancy,' he quipped.

Glatton seemed small in comparison to some of the massive three-deckers in the anchorage, but Oakshott's keen eye detected all the signs of a trim, well-kept command. Small points like the absence of washing hanging out in the heads, gun ports open and freshly painted red on the insides, polished brightwork at the gangway, a newly washed White Ensign fluttering at the mizzen gaff. And when he went aboard, the marine sentries' cross-belts were pipe-clayed and the bugler's instrument positively glittered in the sunlight.

'Come aft, Oakshott,' said Bligh. 'You can sleep in my day cabin and mess with me.'

'Thank you,' responded the other, well aware of the quite considerable sacrifice of comfort the other was making for his benefit.

Long accustomed to small ships, Oakshott had almost forgotten the relative spaciousness enjoyed by the captain of a battleship, even a third-rater like *Glatton*. The day cabin immediately beneath the poop contained a let-down bunk, a collapsible table large enough to seat eight for dinner, desk, chairs galore – and two 12-pounder cannons. The compartment was panelled in light sections of pale green-painted pine that could be struck down and stored during action.

Bligh also had a sleeping cabin for use at sea, which was nearer the companionway up on to the quarter-deck for swift access in emergency.

The two of them dined together that eve off a ragout of salt pork with dried peas and beans, and ship's biscuit. Bligh was not a great drinker and there was no wine, only the usual small beer. It was a pleasant enough meal; the conversation was all about the Service, the European conflict, the coming assault upon Copenhagen. Oakshott was struck with his host's deep professional knowledge. He had known Bligh to be a supreme navigator (how could he be other, having navigated an open boat four thousand miles from the Friendly Islands to Timor in under two months?) whose mentor was the legendary Captain Cook. What impressed him even more was the man's blind and unswerving ethic of leadership. He genuinely held the tenet that a King's Commission, as derived from a King Anointed, carried an authority ordained by Almighty God. It was not a far cry from this philosophy, thought Oakshott, that had brought Bligh to the pass that he suffered aboard *Bounty* – and the need to navigate four thousand miles to stay alive after having driven his men to mutiny.

They turned in early, for Bligh was no night-owl, he attested. The captain's servant made up the bunk, and asked if there was anything that Oakshott required. Yes, it was quite possible to provide Captain Oakshott a glass of brandy from the wardroom pantry.

He drank it in the darkness, sipping gently, seated by an open window of the stern, looking out across the gently heaving sea and the anchored fleet – the nearest being only at a couple of cables' length. From this ship came the sound of a concertina playing what was undoubtedly a hornpipe – though Oakshott was as near tone deaf as made no difference. The fleet was all lit up, and there seemed a vast number of them: the best of Albion's might, poised to make its mark.

Bells from all around marked the hour of eleven: six double clappers. With a sigh, Oakshott drained the last of his brandy, said his prayers, and rolled into the bunk.

He lay awake for quite a while, his thoughts revolving around the cryptic message he had received from Katerina Jacobson – the same that he had carried with him from her very hands at Riga.

He was still thinking about it – and still as confused and puzzled as he had been at first reading it – when sleep overcame him.

The following morning, early, the entire fleet was given the order to weigh anchor and proceed towards Copenhagen, there being a fair wind for the purpose. With the frigates leading and Captain Riou's *Amazon* in the van, the armada sailed down Copenhagen Sound, past Kronborg Castle and Elsinore citadel. They were there subjected to a lively cannonade from the Danish batteries ashore, but Hyde Parker had prudently kept well to the Swedish side of the channel and the fire was ineffective. A few of the British battleships responded but to no discernible effect, save that a burst gun aboard *Isis* caused some casualties, the only ones of the encounter.

At four bells of the forenoon watch, the fleet anchored to the north – and within sight – of Copenhagen, and Hyde Parker and Nelson, accompanied by their staffs, then went on a reconnaissance of the Danish defences aboard Riou's *Amazon*, finding them to have been greatly strengthened since Admiral Dixon's peaceful visit in the previous summer. Apart from the Trekroner batteries, a one-and-a-half-mile line of nineteen warships was moored on the edge of the shallows and covering the eastern side of the city. This in addition to a gathering of moored hulks and rigged ships at the harbour entrance. Add to that, there were the batteries ashore. A formidable prospect for the attackers.

The commander in chief and his subordinates returned to *London* for a council of war in a greatly chastened frame of mind.

All chastened, that is, save Nelson . . .

What the victor of the Nile had seen of the Danish defences had not shaken him one whit from his conviction that a bold and ruthless attack, pressed home at close quarters, would carry the day. It is to his credit, and speaks as much for his powers of persuasion as for his strategic and tactical brilliance, that he carried the waverers – Hyde Parker in particular – and won his point: he was to have *carte blanche* to direct the attack in the manner he determined. To carry this out, the C-in-C gave Nelson twelve battleships – which included Bligh's *Glatton* – and six frigates led by Riou. Nelson had already transferred his flag from *St George* to *Elephant*, which was of a shallower draught and more suitable for inshore sailing.

At just past four bells of the afternoon watch on 1 April Nelson's squadron set sail and, led by Riou's *Amazon*, moved southwards down the narrow channel, to anchor at the end of the Middle Ground shallows. All that was needed now, to begin the battle, was a fair wind from the south, to carry the gallant twelve and their frigates down upon the waiting Danes. And the outlook as regards the wind was propitious.

As soon as the anchor held, Bligh came down to the stern cabin and brusquely demanded a stiff brandy from his servant – an unusual request from one so abstemious. Oakshott joined him. It was apparent to the latter that *Glatton*'s captain was in a highly pent-up state. Presently he revealed the reason for it:

'There are moves afoot, aboard the flagship, to send a boat, or boats, out tonight to test the depths of water between here and the Danish line, Oakshott,' he said. 'I must say that I would give a year of my life – no, I mean it, I assure you – to know if there *is* enough water inshore of the

Danish line to take a ship.' He regarded Oakshott with the light of a zealot in his hazel eyes, and the latter had a brief glimpse of the frenzy that dwelt behind the bland mask of William Bligh.

The fellow was hell-bent to emulate Foley at the Nile: to take his ship inshore of the enemy and have him enveloped on both sides.

Bligh was still speaking . . .

'Yes, I would give a year of my life to have soundings inshore of the Danes. Damn it, I would gladly go myself . . .'

'I'll take a boat out tonight and make those soundings, Bligh,' said Oakshott, knowing full well that it was not lack of courage that held the other back from the enterprise, only the call of duty as ship's captain.

Bligh looked pleased and relieved, and Oakshott guessed that he had hoped for such an offer from him.

'Bravo, Oakshott!' cried *Glatton*'s captain. 'And we'll drink another bumper toast to your venture!'

ELEVEN

Night. The lapping of water on wooden walls. The fleet alight – for what purpose in concealment, when the British ships had surely been under the scrutiny of every spyglass in all Copenhagen and the Danish defences since they arrived off the Middle Ground?

Oakshott had chosen one of the eighteen-foot cutters for the foray, a crew of seven, all armed to the teeth with cutlasses, a pair of pistols per man, and knives. He himself carried his fighting sword, an under-and-over pocket pistol – and a sounding pole that was slightly longer than the boat!

'Good luck, Oakshott!' called Bligh from above.

Oakshott acknowledged with a wave.

'Give way together!'

Muffled oars in greased rowlocks made scarcely a sound as the cutter moved off down the anchorage, just as eight bells from all around tolled the hour of midnight. Less than half a mile ahead the first in the long line of anchored Danes betrayed its presence with an anchor light at the bows.

It was pitch dark, moonless, scarcely a breath of wind, and that coming from the south – a blessing for the morrow.

As they approached the tail of the Middle Ground, Oakshott began to take soundings with the boat's lead and line, and found the five-fathom line very strongly marked. It was here – at a depth of thirty feet – beyond which a battleship proceeded at her peril. He gave the coxswain orders to steer straight towards the lead ship of the Danish line and was soon in the deep water of the narrow channel.

'Keep a sharp eye out for their guard boats,' added Oakshott as they glided down the channel, keeping the Middle Ground on their right hand.

'Aye, aye, sir,' replied the coxswain, Young by name, a veteran of the American War. 'Do we stand and fight if we see one, or do we run, sir?'

'Circumstances will dictate cases,' was the other's reply.

'Aye, *aye*, sir.'

The first Dane was now so close that they could see the carved figurehead of a prancing horse on her stem post, illuminated by the anchor light.

'Young, you will steer well clear of the loom of yonder light,' murmured Oakshott, 'and make for the shore. I shall take soundings of the bottom as close to the line of ships as I may without our being spotted. So gauge your distance and steer accordingly.'

'Aye, aye, sir.'

'From here on, there will be complete silence in the boat.'

Only the faintest whisper of a bow wave could be heard from then on; not a splash of oar or a creak of rowlock served to denote their presence as they passed down the inboard, shore side of the anchored fleet. To their left the city and harbour of Copenhagen rose above the machicolated, dark walls that enclosed the capital. Their eyes having grown accustomed to the darkness, the men in the cutter could see the shape of everything about them, and discern every pinpoint of light, right to the horizon.

Oakshott commenced taking soundings with the long pole – a more prudently silent method than throwing a lead and line.

Abreast of the stern of the leading Dane, he found to his sudden, stirring delight that the pole revealed the depth of four and a half fathoms, in which – with a fair amount of luck – even a three-decker might navigate with caution.

By God, Bligh's supposition was not far amiss, thought

he. If this depth continues much further along the line. And increases . . .

Three oar-strokes further, he took another sounding – and the end of the pole firmly touched bottom at – he felt the incised marks on the pole – two fathoms!

There but for the grace of God was disaster!

He was about to motion the coxswain to turn about and go back the way they had come when there came the sound of voices and the careless plashing of oars and squeak of rowlocks to their right.

A boat had put out from one of the anchored hulks and was coming their way!

The British seamen had scarcely backed oars when the dark shape of another boat of similar size came out of the darkness from the direction of the Danish line. Almost immediately after there came a hail from the other craft – in, presumably, Danish.

'What now, sir?' hissed Young, and there was an eager, fighting lilt in his voice.

'Be still,' murmured Oakshott. 'Sit quietly in your thwarts, lads. Pistols and cutlasses at the ready, but don't shoot till I give the order.'

The hail from the other boat was repeated, but not with any note of hostility – or even of urgency.

Oakshott and Young were conscious of this nuance, both. 'I reckon they think we're one o' them, sir,' said the latter. 'An' they're just wishing us "good night", like.'

'It's possible,' said Oakshott. 'In any event, we'll assume that – for the time being – in the hope that they just pass us by. We are not well placed to start a fight.' He looked across at the looming black shape of the battle line. 'Too many neighbours!'

The hail was repeated yet again, and then the other craft changed course so as to come straight at them.

'Stand by, lads!' murmured Oakshott, and he cocked the first barrel of his under-and-over.

As the newcomer drew closer it could be seen that there were two oarsmen, each pulling at two sculls. And there were about five passengers huddled in a dark mass in the stern sheets. The two crews were evenly matched. Oakshott had almost decided to cut down the odds with a quick broadside of pistolry at long range when someone called to them again in Danish. And now there was no doubt about it: by the tone of voice, by the lilt and inflection of the words, one could have sworn that what they had heard was a comradely greeting.

'Hold your fire,' breathed Oakshott. 'I fancy they're going to come alongside – in which case they're in for a surprise.'

Oakshott never spoke a truer word – though the surprise, when it came, was mutual . . .

The other boat bumped alongside. Hands reached out to pull them close together. Someone in the stern sheets of the other craft struck a flint. A lantern was lit amidst a buzz of decidedly non-hostile conversation.

The scene was illuminated – in a shocked silence from all present . . .

What the Danes saw was a line of levelled pistols, the glint of drawn steel, and seven scowling countenances suddenly wide-eyed with surprise.

The Britishers gazed upon two unarmed oarsmen, a uniformed coxswain at the tiller – also unarmed. And sitting in the stern sheets, a bevy of four female persons whom even the most charitable would have designated – from their paint and patches, their frizzed coiffures, the scandalous cut of their bodices and the lurid coloration of the frocks they wore – to be ladies of the town.

'Good Gawd!' exclaimed one of *Glatton*'s boat's crew, speaking for them all, Oakshott included, 'it's just a boatload of whores bein' taken back ashore!'

One of the Britishers – young and nervous, perhaps – raised his pistol aggressively, but Oakshott knocked it down. His gaze swept over the faces of the four frightened women and he met the eyes of the coxswain, who was carrying the lantern.

'Douse that damned light!' snapped he, pointing.

Whether the man understood English or not, Oakshott's intention was very clear. Lifting the lantern, the former blew it out. In the darkness that followed, one could almost sense the wave of relief from the ladies of the night.

'Fend off,' murmured Oakshott, 'and give way together. Back to *Glatton* we go!'

Like ships that make a passing encounter in the dark hours, the cargo of dockyard strumpets and the boatload of armed Britishers went on their way unharmed and unharming. And Oakshott smiled to himself in the darkness.

Two facts he had clearly established that night: first, the Danes were in good spirits and making full use of the local amenities; second, Nelson's line of battle would never pass inshore of the enemy line.

There would be no second Nile on the morrow; the battle, whichever other turn it took, would be unique in the annals of naval warfare.

The following morning, shortly before four bells of the forenoon watch on 2 April 1801, Nelson gave the signal for his squadron to weigh anchor in a prearranged succession. First to proceed was *Edgar*, 74 guns. As she passed down the line, she was greeted with resounding cheers from her associates. Oakshott and Bligh watched her pass close by as they stood together on *Glatton*'s quarter-deck.

'A brave sight, Oakshott,' said the other. 'There's nothing so becomes a battle as the beginning of it.' Bligh knew what he was talking about: he wore the king's gold medal for his services at the Battle of Camperdown. 'The aftermath is often not so splendid,' he added.

'Hyde Parker's moving,' said Oakshott, pointing to the

north where three distant sail were tacking towards the Trekroner. The C-in-C was up at the northern anchorage and ready to give support to Nelson's southern attack.

'The less Sir Hyde interferes in this engagement, the better for Nelson and us to get on with the business in hand,' growled Bligh, snapping shut his telescope.

All around them ships were shaking out their sails and taking the wind as their anchors came up. *Ardent*, 74, followed after *Edgar*, and *Glatton*'s turn came next.

'I have to report, sir, that all guns are run out and ready to fire on the port side,' said Oakshott, gunnery officer.

'Very good, Oakshott,' responded Bligh. Then, unbending slightly, he added: 'Your soundings inboard of the Danish line were well received by his Lordship, so I'm told.' The ghost of a smile flitted across his handsome, austere countenance. 'It's to be hoped that the Danes are wearied after their exertions with the ladies of the town, and lying late abed this morning.'

'They were most potential-looking ladies,' grinned Oakshott.

'Anchor's a-trip, sir!' From the fo'c's'le.

Followed almost immediately after by: *'Anchor's aweigh, sir!'*

The ship creaked like an old corset as her sails took the wind and bore her slowly forward, with every rope and every piece of timber aboard her adjusting to the movement.

'Take station astern of *Ardent*,' ordered Bligh.

Oakshott went to the taffrail and looked back. One by one, Nelson's division was coming to sail and forming rough line in the order which the admiral had ordained in the instructions he had dictated aloud till after midnight the previous night, to be transcribed by half a dozen clerks and delivered to the ships before dawn.

Gradually, the line took shape: *Isis* and Nelson's old command *Agamemnon*; *Bellona*, *Elephant* and *Ganges*;

Monarch, *Defiance*, *Russell* and *Polyphemus*. And Riou's flotilla of frigates.

With a fair wind bearing the twelve battleships and their consorts in good order towards the inner channel and the waiting Danes, Oakshott took the opportunity to go below and see how things were faring on the gundecks.

He found the men in high spirits, imbued with a fighting determination to get to grips with the enemy, and loud in their praises of Captain Bligh. In his brief stay aboard *Glatton* Oakshott had noticed that, whilst Bligh was popular on the lower deck, there was a distinct frigidity shown to him by his officers. On reflection, it was to be remembered that the *Bounty* mutiny was caused to a large extent by her captain's overbearing manner towards the officers and subordinate officers of his command (the notorious ringleader of the mutiny, Fletcher Christian, was master's mate), and the mutiny was very much a 'palace revolution'.

'Orders for loading, sir?' requested the gun captain of one of the potent carronades, knuckling his forelock with a fierce look in his eye.

Mindful that, if all went well, they would be shooting at a range of something less than two hundred yards when *Glatton* reached her designated station, Oakshott felt free to humour the fellow. 'When it comes to the pounding match, we will likely be double, or even treble-shotted,' he said. 'But we must wait and see.'

'Treble-shotted!'

'Hoo-rah for *Glatton* and Cap'n Bligh!' The cry went up. 'And hoo-rah for Cap'n Oakshott!'

Smilingly acknowledging their cheers, Oakshott went on his way to the lower deck, past the marine sentries who stood at the top of the companionway with bayonets fixed, to dissuade any hand who took fright and tried to hide below. It was scarcely to be believed that there was any such man – or boy – in all the crew who would stoop to such conduct; from grizzled veteran to midshipman and powder monkey scarcely aged in double figures, Oakshott saw nothing but fighting spirit and enthusiasm.

The massive 32-pounders of the lower deck were ready and loaded, fore to aft, port and starboard. As Nelson had ordained, the battle was to be fought with his squadron anchored by the stern with their port sides facing the enemy at close range. Oakshott's order as gunnery officer – and approved by Bligh – was that the batteries on the starboard, disengaged side were to be loaded with powder and ball, but not pricked and primed, so that if for any reason *Glatton* had to go about, the starboard batteries could swiftly engage. Meanwhile, the eight-men starboard crews of the lower deck – like those of the 12-pounders and carronades above – were at hand to replace the comrades who would fall when the enemy ball came crashing in through the wooden walls, to turn the gundecks into slaughter-houses of flying steel and slivered oak.

His inspection complete, Oakshott went up top again – in time to see Bligh and the others on the quarter-deck looking abaft and pointing with great consternation.

'What's amiss?' asked Oakshott of a midshipman.

'Sir, *Agamemnon* has gone aground,' piped the lad.

Sure enough. Fifth in the somewhat ragged line, Nelson's old command, straying too far to starboard, had struck bottom at the tail of the Middle Ground where Oakshott had taken lead and line soundings the previous night, putting her in the same humiliating position that *Culloden* had occupied at the Nile three years previously.

Meanwhile, the lead ship *Edgar* was already coming under fire from the head of the Danish line. The battle was joined.

Bligh was a mountain of calm, the imminence of action and danger seeming to have quenched the restless spirit within him. He approached Oakshott and held out his hand.

'Good luck to you today, my dear fellow,' he said. 'I hope

we may both take wine this evening in celebration of a famous victory. In any event, we'll make a fine clatter before the day's out.

'One thing more,' he went on. 'If I am hit, you will assume command of the ship, not only on the score of seniority over my number one, but because of the high regard in which I have come to hold you during our very short acquaintance.'

They shook hands and Oakshott thanked him, well aware of the effort it must have cost a man so reserved and inward-looking to have unburdened himself so freely. They then parted company: Bligh to his place by the wheel, where he could con the ship to its allotted place in the firing line; Oakshott to the head of the gangway leading down to the upper gundeck, where he could both observe the progress of the battle and pass orders down to the officers of quarters – or hurry on down below in case of an emergency.

The wind was fickle. The great ships moved with tantalizing slowness towards their destiny of fire. *Edgar* had already been hit and was returning shot for shot. Drifting white gunsmoke obscured the next in line – *Ardent* – from Oakshott's view, but he reckoned that she must be almost abreast of the leading Dane. It wanted only minutes before *Glatton* would be in action.

As on every similar occasion that he could remember – the brief span of peace before action – Oakshott experienced something akin to the legendary vision of past life that is supposed to flash before the mind of a drowning person. His first thought was of the beloved mother who had been taken from him far too soon and had left a hole in his being that nothing – and certainly no other woman – had ever adequately filled. The train of thought naturally led him to Irene Chancellor who, by every yardstick of rank and fortune, should by now have become his wife, but had not for reasons he was unable to define. Inevitably, there arose the image of his sister-in-law, who certainly would have taken him to her if asked. He wondered if her second child was girl or boy, and hoped that Mr Henry Jarvis was treating her well.

All of which brought his mind to a point that he had been deliberately evading ever since his first night aboard *Glatton* – the affair that he had had with Katerina Jacobson. And the letter that still reposed in his coat-tail pocket. A letter which, should he be killed in the coming action, would join him over the side when they cleared away the detritus of the carnage and continued with the task in hand . . .

Someone was calling to him.

'Stand by to give fire, Captain Oakshott!' from Bligh.

'Aye, aye!' He acknowledged with a wave. The gunfire was now close and deafening; it would get worse.

Putting a speaking trumpet to his lips, Oakshott ducked below the companionway coaming and gave the order to the nearest officer of quarters: *'Pass the word to give fire in a rolling volley when your guns bear!'*

Through the swirling gunsmoke Oakshott then saw the prow of the leading Danish ship, prancing lion figurehead and all, as it began to slip slowly towards *Glatton*'s long bowsprit. Almost in the same breath a majestic calm descended upon his spirits, and he knew – for the umpteenth time with an unshakable and unquestioned certainty – that this was what he was born for, this his destiny, and like to be his end.

No need to repeat the order: as soon as *Glatton*'s prow was abreast of the prancing lion, her two gundecks spoke out: 32-pounder cannon and 68-pound carronade speaking in duet, and repeated, and repeated, and repeated right down the line of moving gun ports. The din was shocking to the ears and the senses, the stench of burnt powder curiously pleasant if one had developed a taste for it. (And mightily good for congestion of the chest; bronchitis was almost unheard of in a fighting ship.)

Almost immediately after, the first of the enemy's shot came inboard. Fired at waterline level, the Danes' first salvoes took *Glatton* from there on upwards. The screams of wounded and dying men came to Oakshott's ears along the narrow funnel of the gundeck and the companionway, but he was too busy observing the fall of his own shot to pay heed to that.

It seemed to him that some more weight could with advantage be added to his fire.

'Pass the word - double shot your next loading!' he shouted through the trumpet. The officer of quarters acknowledged with a wave, and the order was repeated mouth to mouth along both gundecks, before Oakshott had scarcely lowered the trumpet.

The concerted din, the smoke, the stink, gave an air of total unreality to the action. Down below, men already sweating from their efforts toiled half-naked at their arduous tasks: swabbing out wet and dry, ramming and re-ramming; the powder monkeys scurrying to and from the magazine with their cased charges of gunpowder; former farmers' lads from Suffolk and Northumberland, Jamaica and Ontario vying with each other to be first to give fire; languid fops turned officers praying for a chance of distinction - they were all at it. All save the dead, who were already being bundled unceremoniously out of the gun ports whenever the pieces were run in for reloading.

Oakshott counted each Dane that slid past his vision, remarking to himself how their rate of fire was discernibly slower than was normally acceptable in the Royal Navy. But there was no faulting the accuracy of their shooting: at a little under two hundred yards, balls were coming in-board in fair number, and the mainsail immediately for'ard of where he stood on the top step of the companionway was riddled like a colander with holes the size of a baby's head.

The progress along the Danish line was slow. Not till eleven o'clock that morning did *Glatton* pass between the anchored *Edgar* and the Danish line, and drop her hook in precisely the spot that Nelson had ordained for her: a cable's length – one hundred and seventy-five yards as near as damn it – from the Danish flagship *Dannebrog*.

It was a key position: Nelson knew a navigator and a ship-handler when he saw one.

The progress of the battle for Copenhagen – most of which went unseen by Oakshott, as by any other man fighting there, be he British or Danish, for those most intimately involved in killing and not being killed see so very little beyond the scope of their own interests – was inexpressibly brutal.

Nelson's plan of attack had basic parallels with his method at the Nile. The part of the enemy line least easily to be reinforced was to be overcome in the first assault. He had in mind to destroy utterly the first half-dozen moored vessels up to the flagship *Dannebrog*. To this end, he originally concentrated the leading battleships of his line. However, with *Agamemnon* going aground, and also *Russell* and *Bellona* – all on the tail of the Middle Ground – his assault force was cut by one quarter almost before the battle was truly joined.

By midday, however, the last of the British line – *Defiance* – was in place close by the Trekroner batteries. And the killing match for Copenhagen was on.

The ordeals endured by some of the British ships and their crews almost defy credibility. *Monarch*, commanded by Captain J.R. Mosse, received the most appalling punishment of all. Taking the place in the battle line that had been apportioned to the grounded *Russell*, Mosse ended up within range of a hulk called *Sjaelland* and also the Trekroner. Mosse himself was killed in the first broadside that swathed across his upper deck as *Monarch* came to anchor and was laid out in his own stern walk under a flag, so that his hard-pressed men should not see that their captain was gone during the long and terrible afternoon that followed.

The misfortunes of *Bellona*, captained by Sir Thomas Thompson, Bart, were many and various. In addition to going aground and consequently missing her station, *Bellona* was placed well inside gun range of the Danish line, yet was herself stuck in such a position that she was unable to bring her broadside to bear. In addition to that, the ship – one of the oldest in the fleet – had been supplied with faulty cannon whose metal was honeycombed with air pockets, with the result that such firing as she was able to contrive was insidiously fatal to herself, for in the early afternoon one of the guns on the lower deck burst, killing and wounding several men, including two lieutenants and two midshipmen; the explosion also causing one of the main-deck beams and part of the main-deck gangway to collapse. Shortly after, another gun on the same deck burst, killing and wounding more men and blowing up part of the main deck above, as well as disabling five of the guns up there. Sir Thomas himself – a veteran of the Nile when captain of *Leander* – was wounded quite early on in the battle, when a shot took off his left leg and he was carried below, his life and career ruined – a fate that had always haunted Charles Oakshott.

There were follies a-plenty amidst the valour and the gallantry. One of the ships was carrying soldiers who were to form a landing party and storm the city when the Danish fleet had been overcome. The commanding officer of this party, inquiring of the ship's captain where his men should be stationed during the battle, was told that, since they could be of no possible use in a killing match with cannon, they had best shelter below till their turn came. The response of this gentleman was that such a thing was impossible, since it would reek of cowardice and bring upon them a disgrace that could never be wiped out. Accordingly, he had his soldiers drawn up at the gangway as if on parade, to satisfy his cruel point of honour, and they were mown down – decimated – where they stood to attention, by grapeshot. And all to no purpose. The mindless pride of a fool was paramount.

Aboard the flagship, Nelson, knowing that the issue was very much in the balance, maintained his customary calm and fortitude, rebuking an excited lieutenant who had reported the grounding of *Russell* and *Bellona* in a manner which he regarded as defeatist. But in truth, the battle was touch and go after three hours of hard pounding – though even Nelson was not to know that the corner was already turned, and the Danish resistance was just about to break.

It was at this crucial moment that Nelson's flag lieutenant reported a signal from the C-in-C, lying at anchor to the north:

Discontinue the engagement.

'Discontinue the *engagement?*'

Oakshott and Bligh were together on the quarter-deck when the signal was reported to them, the former having joined the ship's captain to report on the state in the gundecks. They stared at each other in utter puzzlement.

'The old man's mad!' was Bligh's summation. 'Why, to up anchor and sail on down the enemy line before the wind – and there's no other way to go – would be to commit suicide. We'd be whipped like runaway curs.'

'Is Nelson repeating the signal?' asked Oakshott.

This was the crucial question, for *Glatton*, like the rest of the squadron, took orders only through their immediate superior – that is, Nelson in *Elephant*.

'*Elephant* doesn't respond, sir,' said the flag midshipman.

Oakshott and Bligh exchanged grim glances.

'He wouldn't dare,' murmured the latter, *sotto voce*. 'Not even *he* would disregard a direct command.'

'That remains to be seen,' countered Oakshott.

A whole five minutes passed, and then a flag hoist rose slowly and remained at *Elephant*'s main topsail yardarm – prominently displayed for all to see . . .

'Admiral Nelson is acknowledging the signal from the commander in chief, sir!'

'Nothing more?' demanded Bligh. 'The order isn't being repeated?'

'No, sir.'

It was an act of open defiance, and not Nelson's first. By merely acknowledging the signal he took it upon himself to order his captains to turn the same blind eye upon Hyde Parker's flag hoist as he himself had done.

Tragically, there were some in the squadron – distanced from *Elephant* and under the eye of Hyde Parker – who instantly obeyed the signal to disengage. Riou of *Amazon* was the first to do so. This gallant and distinguished captain was engaging the Trekroner batteries which he and Oakshott had first seen, and gauged their might, that memorable night of the reception at the Christiansborg palace.

Riou turned his frigate away from the battery with great regret, commenting: 'What will Nelson think of us?' He then joined in assisting a party of marines to haul on the main-brace under heavy fire, with the words: 'Come on, my boys, let's all die together.' This injunction had scarcely passed his lips when a fatal shot severed him in two. In one instant, the Royal Navy was deprived of one of its finest captains.

Amazon's withdrawal under murderous fire was seen from *Glatton*. But, of course, they had no knowledge of Riou's fate. Indeed, both Bligh and Oakshott had become aware – most stirringly aware – that the Danish fire had begun to falter shortly after Nelson's acknowledgement of Parker's signal. Moreover, one of the floating batteries at the end of the Danish line cut her cables and made for harbour, sinking as she went.

Glatton who, together with *Elephant*, had been pouring

fire into *Dannebrog*, was in a unique position to speed the course of the enemy's defeat.

William Bligh was quick to perceive this.

He addressed Oakshott, pointing to the Danish flagship.

'Kill that ship, Oakshott!' he cried. 'Kill her stone dead!'

'Aye, aye, sir,' breathed the other, and went to do Bligh's bidding.

'Pass the word – all guns reload – triple-shotted!'

The order was passed, and cannon and carronade, packed almost to the muzzle with propellant powder and polished iron ball, were discharged at the Danish flagship. At that close range there was no need to increase the powder to a dangerous degree, merely to increase the elevation, so that the triple shots struck home from a higher trajectory.

The results were devastating. One needs only to imagine – in the case of the carronade, supremely well adapted for close-range pounding – the effect of one cataclysmic impact of over two hundred pounds of plunging iron from a single piece, and this multiplied by six and augmented by lighter shot, the whole arriving home in one-minute cycles, to have some idea of the devastation wrought aboard the *Dannebrog*. And this is not counting what she was receiving from *Elephant*'s 37-gun broadsides.

Half an hour after Hyde Parker's futile signal nearly all the Danish ships and batteries had ceased fire, and Nelson deemed that troops could be landed to take over the dockyard and arsenal. However, the shore batteries, still in substantially sound condition, poured fire upon the boats which had put out to board the ships which had struck their colours, and the British line, which had ceased firing, was forced to open up again – causing indescribable havoc in the battered hulks. In less time than it takes to tell, *Dannebrog* broke free of her moorings and was drifting away downwind.

At about two bells in the first dog watch, she blew up, taking the larger part of her crew with her.

It was then that Nelson, with his often-proclaimed policy of mercy after victory, wrote a note to the prince royal, nominal commander of the Danish Forces, begging His Highness, in the name of humanity and the long-established kinship that exists between Danes and Englishmen, to order a cease fire and surrender. After only requesting some clarification of the terms of surrender, the prince agreed, and the firing ceased on both sides.

The Battle of Copenhagen – fought grudgingly and for the worst of all possible reasons – was won.

The guns secured, Oakshott came up on deck. Face blackened, hatless, his hair caked with burnt powder, the white facings of his borrowed uniform coat streaked with filth and other men's blood, he was scarcely recognized by Bligh – who was in a like condition.

Bligh, who had just narrowly evaded a multiple collision between *Monarch* and *Ganges*, involving *Defiance* and *Elephant* – the two latter ships having gone aground in the resultant hugger-mugger – looked about at the end of his tether.

'It was a hard day's work, Oakshott,' said he. 'And, as I mentioned earlier, there's not much splendour in the aftermath of a battle.'

Oakshott nodded, leaning against the mizzen chains and looking out across Copenhagen roads at the smoking, battered hulks, the mastless ships, the drifting debris of masts, sail and cordage. And, floating everywhere – bodies, bodies, bodies . . .

'When all the diplomacy has failed,' he mused, 'when kings and princes have had their little say, and when it is all over, it's poor Jack Tar who's paid the butcher's bill!'

TWELVE

The day following the battle Nelson went ashore and was received by the prince royal. The little admiral, scorning the use of a carriage, walked through the crowded streets with only the officers of his staff about him, and was greeted by the Danes with neither adulation nor disfavour, but with the respect accorded to a brave and humane victor.

Aboard *Glatton* – as among most of the fleet not concerned with extricating themselves from being aground – there was a make-do-and-mend, which is the Royal Navy's immemorial euphemism for doing absolutely nothing but getting one's head down.

The following morning Oakshott gathered together his few possessions and sought out Bligh. The latter had also just risen and was writing up his report in the ship's log. He looked up and smiled when the other entered.

'You're leaving us, Oakshott,' he said.

'I've much to settle, Bligh,' said Oakshott. 'It seems to me that, being nominally under Lord Nelson's command, I should report aboard *Elephant* and get some orders, whatever they may be. Personally, I should like to take steps to free *Javelin*, since we still do not seem to be at war with Russia – and yesterday's efforts may go far to prevent that lunatic tsar from throwing in his lot with the godless French.'

Bligh nodded. 'I wish you all good fortune, Oakshott,' he said. 'And thanks for your support. I wish you well in recovering your ship.' The hazel eyes flickered away and looked into scenes that were privy only to him. 'It is a terrible thing to lose one's ship, Oakshott. A terrible thing.'

He was still staring into the middle distance when Oakshott left him.

Amid the turmoil of the battle's aftermath it was some hours before Oakshott was able to secure a boat to take him to Nelson's flagship which, having been hauled off the Middle Ground, had joined Hyde Parker at the northern anchorage. He was received aboard there with some civility but precious little assistance.

Said the officer of the day: 'His lordship has only just finished breakfast, and at the present time is receiving some of his senior captains. I'm sure, sir, that if you were to wait in the wardroom, his lordship's secretary will attend to your needs when he is free.'

Oakshott thanked him and went aft. He had not gone further than the quarter-deck screen when he was accosted by a face that was familiar from the recent past.

'Lord Charles, sir. How are you? What a very pleasant coincidence.'

The speaker was young, irremediably good-looking – despite the bandage that half-covered his face. His right arm, also, was bandaged and slung.

Oakshott pointed at him. 'Mr Walker!' he declared. 'Flag lieutenant to Admiral Dixon.'

'*Former* flagloot, sir,' grinned the other. 'I volunteered to join his lordship just as soon as the Baltic expedition was mooted. I said to myself, "That's where the advancement lies!"' His bland, still unformed countenance was free of all guile, there was only enthusiasm present. 'But what' – he made an expressive gesture encompassing Oakshott's far from prepossessing appearance – 'What have you been about, sir, if one may be so bold? One has heard about *Javelin*, but . . .'

Oakshott cut him short. 'Mr Walker,' he said, 'what I

most need is to see Lord Nelson. I've no wish to cool my heels whilst some functionary makes up his mind to condescend to grant me an audience. You must know the ropes in the flagship. What do you suggest?'

Walker was not one whit put about. His pleasant face broadened into a heartening beam. 'Why, sir, I have just come from the admiral,' he said, 'and he's in a most accommodating frame of mind. Come with me, sir, and together we'll cut through the mealy-mouthed protocol of grubby functionaries.' So saying, he led Oakshott under the quarter-deck screen to the holy of holies that lay at the far end of the upper deck. And there, after tapping upon the door, he opened it to admit Oakshott.

'Admiral,' he said, 'may I present Captain Lord Charles Oakshott of *Javelin*?'

It was not only the brash, irresistible charm of the egregious Walker that carried the day – of this Oakshott was well aware. The little admiral, halfway through a dissertation to the three officers present with him, paused in mid-sentence, his hand poised in mid-air, and flashed a glance towards the newcomers.

'Aaah – Oakshott!' he cried. 'Thank God that you have survived the battle – and whole and hearty, as I perceive you.

'Gentlemen, you will have met Oakshott when he was aboard last. Oakshott – to refresh your memory – Captains Foley, Fremantle and Fancourt.

'Thank you, Mr Walker. You may leave us.'

Nelson's expressive lips pursed in a smile as he watched Walker go out and close the door behind him. 'That young sprig, gentlemen,' said he, 'who on first sight appears to be little more than a salon gallant in naval uniform, bore himself most honourably in the battle, as officer of quarters on the upper deck. When one of the guns' crews was decimated, he assisted in serving the piece whilst under heavy fire. I shall mention him in my dispatch, and I've no doubt but that the patriotic Fund will grant him a medal or a presentation sword.' The admiral's expression changed. 'Ah, but we have lost some good men, gentlemen. Riou – I can scarcely bring myself to speak of his going. If that signal had not been sent . . .

'And Mosse – brave, stubborn Mosse. How we shall miss him. Thompson – now I shall go to see him at an early opportunity. They tell me he is very low . . .

'Oakshott, I was telling the others about my meeting with the prince royal, and how the populace greeted me with what only can be described as a mixture of curiosity and admiration, mixed with a touch of pleasure. The prince and I spoke together very freely. It is to be hoped that the poor wreck who is his father may soon be mercifully gathered in, and the son succeed to the crown of Denmark.

'His Highness very cannily put it to me: "Why has the British fleet come to the Baltic?" and I replied, "For to crush a most formidable and unprovoked coalition against Great Britain." This led the prince to declare that nothing would ever make him take a part against Great Britain.' Nelson smiled. 'I cannot help thinking, gentlemen, that our work of the day before yesterday did much to concentrate His Highness's mind upon that decision!'

Expressions of agreement greeted the admiral's quip, and a general conversation followed, during which servants brought in coffee and Bath Oliver biscuits. Cup and saucer in hand, Oakshott presently found himself side by side with Nelson.

'Well now, my dear fellow, you will be looking for fresh employment, I don't doubt,' said the latter. 'And it is for this you have come to see me. Do I have it aright?'

'Indeed you do, sir,' responded Oakshott. 'And the employment I most earnestly seek is to resume active command of my ship.'

Nelson nodded. 'I think I see a strategy with which this may be brought about, Oakshott,' he said. 'A dispatch boat is leaving for St Petersburg today with a memorandum which is at present being cobbled together in the fleet flagship by Sir Hyde in consultation with his political advisers. I may say that I have already given my view upon the composition of the memorandum. Briefly, it will inform Tsar Paul that as a result of our labours of the day before yesterday he can discount Denmark from his calculations – and Norway and Sweden also. The news may influence the tsar in great things and in small: he may break off his intrigues with Bonaparte; and he may free the British ships he is holding – including *Javelin*.'

Oakshott thought he saw the way Nelson's mind was working, but just to make sure, he drew a deep breath and began:

'Sir, if I may be so bold . . .'

He got no further. 'Yes, you will certainly travel in that dispatch boat, Oakshott,' said the victor of Copenhagen. 'And I earnestly pray that you may return with your ship.'

Almost as if in imitation – or jealous resentment – of the fury that had been unleashed on 2 April, the tutelary gods of the Baltic Sea called down tempest and torment upon the dispatch schooner *Pickle* as she set off northwards to St Petersburg. For two days and three nights the well-found little ship battled against everything which that notoriously fickle sea could mount against the incursions of mere man.

Oakshott, a stranger to seasickness, ate doggedly and alone in the tiny saloon aft that served as a wardroom for the captain and two officers; the others preferred to lie in their bunks and suffer in comfort, when they were not suffering in gross discomfort on watch on the wave-swept upper deck. Oakshott obligingly stood watch with the others, which was greatly appreciated. On this, the third day out, he had consumed a hearty breakfast of gammon and eggs and soft tommy, when there came a hail from above:

'Sail ho! Dead ahead!'

Downing a mouthful of laced cocoa, Oakshott grabbed his oilskins and climbed up on deck, shrugging them on as he went.

HMS *Pickle*'s commander, one Lieutenant Bradshawe, was keeping the forenoon watch on the quarter-deck, where two quartermasters handled the long steering tiller. He pointed out through the murk ahead, where the eye of faith could just discern the topsails of a full-rigged ship on the horizon when she rose above the troughs.

'She's a frigate I think, sir!' yelled Bradshawe over the howling of the wind. 'And coming straight at us!'

'One of ours, or a Frog, I wonder?' speculated Oakshott.

'We'll soon see. If a Frog, we turn and run. There isn't a frigate built that could catch *Pickle* going close-hauled.'

Bracing himself against the mainmast shrouds, Oakshott waited with interest to learn the identity of the oncoming stranger, careless of the seas that broke over *Pickle*'s bow and swept right along her deck every time her elegant bowsprit dipped into white water. No one but he amongst those off watch had summoned up enough interest – or energy – to come on deck in response to the sail-ho.

The minutes slipped past. Now one could see the stranger's topsails all the time, very soon the mainsails also. One of the quartermasters – having better eyes than the rest of them – let out a whoop of delight to see the White Ensign streaming at the other's mizzen gaff.

'She's one of ours!'

It was then – like the beginning of a beloved tune played upon a well-tempered instrument – that Oakshott became slowly aware of the identity of the ship ahead . . .

The set of the sails was curiously familiar.

The bowsprit – pitched a little more rakishly than most, but that was after the original bowsprit was lost in Lucky Jimmy's madcap foray.

And the silhouette, when the whole of her came, like a bride to her awaiting groom, to his adoring eyes . . .

'By God – it's *Javelin!*'

There was no hope of lowering a boat to go across to her, madness to attempt to go alongside in the raging seas. All he could do was to wave and shout – fruitlessly – at the figures on deck as the two vessels wallowed together at a safe distance.

Oakshott endured the frustration of waving and shouting pointlessly at the figures on *Javelin*'s quarter-deck: at Tom Brewster with his hat jammed down tightly over his ears and ostrich feathers flying; Pepe Lopez, dapper as ever in clerical grey cloak; many others. And a portly figure of a man who beyond all belief could be none other than Consul-General Constantinopolous.

The wind and sea abated during the afternoon, and *Javelin* was first to lower a boat. Gathering together his few traps, Oakshott said goodbye to his hosts and climbed down over the side, to be received by waiting hands.

'Welcome back, sir,' said Midshipman Cobbold, who seemed to have filled out admirably during his confinement in Narva.

The boisterous sea kept Cobbold busy at his tiller and precluded Oakshott from throwing even the basic questions at him concerning the ship's presence in mid-Baltic. Not till he had climbed back aboard his own command and received the salutes, the pipes, the hand-wringings and the cheers of his crew, was he able to draw breath and put it to them:

'How in hell did you get away?' he demanded.

'Sir, we were released and told to go,' replied Brewster.

'There was a great flurry in Narva. Soldiers everywhere, sir . . .'

'At first we thought that Russia had declared war on us, sir . . .'

'And then the news was everywhere, sir . . .'

'The Tsar Paul has been assassinated, Oakshott.'

The last speaker was Consul-General Constantinopolous. And he added: 'Russia's dalliance with godless France and Bonaparte is ended!'

With a delicacy that well became him, Tom Brewster had not installed himself in his captain's stern cabin during the long internment, and servant Bantock had availed himself of his time to make widespread improvements: he had painted the panelling near to the new pale green inspired by the Etruria pottery and widely adopted by the navy. From somewhere he had obtained a bolt of striped silk and re-covered the chairs; the teak deck shone like a dance floor, and was further embellished by a pair of oriental rugs from heaven knows where.

Oakshott sat down at table with Brewster, Pepe Lopez and Constantinopolous.

'Consul-General. Gentlemen,' said Oakshott. 'Before you flesh out *your* news, I must tell you that Lord Nelson has won a massive victory at Copenhagen!'

There was a stir around the table.

He went on: 'The Danish fleet is no longer in being, and Norway, Sweden and Denmark do not now pose either a threat to Great Britain, or offer any hope of an alliance to Russia and the French.'

He waited till the excitement had died down and he had answered divers questions about the battle and his part in it. He then turned to Constantinopolous. 'Mr Consul-General,' he said. 'You have the floor. Tell me all that has happened since I saw you last, I beg you.'

Constantinopolous inclined his well-barbered head. 'With the greatest of pleasure, Captain,' he said. 'Firstly, as you have been informed, the Tsar Paul was assassinated – strangled by a person or persons close to him. Holy Russia is now ruled by his son Alexander – a confirmed Anglophile and a hater of Bonaparte and all his works. I do not know, I can only guess, what effect Lord Nelson's victory will have upon the general policy of the Baltic states, but it is certain that Paul's grandiose schemes – as set out in the correspondence that you yourself smuggled out of Narva with the help of Countess Jacobson – have died with him.'

Mention of Katerina Jacobson still had the power to arouse Oakshott to obscure passions. Thrusting the image of her aside, he asked: 'What exactly was in that dispatch – the copies of those letters between Bonaparte and Tsar Paul that Axel Bernstorff abstracted?'

'Potent stuff,' said Constantinopolous. 'Paul proposed among other things to join with Bonaparte in persuading Portugal, Spain and even the United States of America to the Armed Neutrality.'

'The devil he did!'

'He also suggested to Bonaparte that, with French support, both military and diplomatic, Russia should invade India.'

'By God – the hands that dispatched the Tsar Paul performed a service to all Europe, and beyond!' declared Oakshott. 'But who was the assassin, or assassins?'

Constantinopolous flashed a glance at Lopez and Brewster.

'By your leave, sir,' he said, 'that question touches on matters which are too confidential to be widely disseminated. I would prefer that you repeat your question when we are alone together.'

Oakshott nodded. 'Very well.

'And now, gentlemen, I have been very remiss as a host. Will you not now join me in a bumper of brandy to mark my return?'

Past midday . . .

Oakshott was entertaining Constantinopolous to luncheon *à deux*. The dispatch schooner *Pickle* could be seen through the stern windows as she went on her way to St Petersburg with the news for the new tsar that his late father's grandiose schemes had been largely set to naught in the Copenhagen roads. The sight of the fast-receding sails prompted Oakshott to a line of thought . . .

'You tell me, Consul-General, that Tsar Paul was assassinated on March twenty-fourth. Now, there is a savage irony here, for this was a week and more before the battle. It is likely that, if news of the assassination had reached Hyde Parker, the assault upon Copenhagen might have been abandoned as a superfluity.'

'It is entirely possible, and rightly so,' said the Greek. 'But you see, my dear fellow, the person or persons who planned and carried out the assassination had – so to speak – two strings to their bow. On the one hand, the receipt of the Bonaparte letters in London would almost certainly cause Britain to act precipitately against the Armed Neutrality.

'On the other hand . . .' He left the issue in the air.

'On the other hand,' said Oakshott, 'our conspirator – or conspirators – settled the question by using the other string to their bow – the assassination of the tsar!

'And who was behind all this, Constantinopolous?'

'Count Axel Bernstorff,' replied the other. 'Who else?'

At that juncture Bantock came in to clear away the dessert plates and bring in fruit, nuts and port. A sharp glance from his master told the sensitively alerted servant that his presence must not be long protracted, and he was out of the door again in very swift order.

'Do you have really hard evidence for that supposition, Consul-General?' asked Oakshott, pouring the port.

'I do, my friend,' responded the other. 'And I intend to present the same to Mr Pitt in person, together with my summation of the Russian situation in general.'

'Not Mr Pitt,' said Oakshott. 'Pitt has resigned and Addington has taken his place – rather inadequately, by common opinion. There is a little verse going the rounds . . .

'Pitt is to Addington
As London is to Paddington.'

He was mildly amused to see that, for all his cosmopolitanism, the point of the jingle was lost on the sophisticated Greek.

'Well then, to Addington I shall address myself,' said the other. 'You ask me what evidence I have. Well – I must tell you that his sister, the charming baroness with whom we are both well acquainted, confessed to me that, in addition to obtaining copies of the Bonaparte correspondence, her brother had set in train a plot to assassinate the tsar. It was her wish, her desperate wish, to prevent him from this extreme course. In order to do this, she proposed to travel to St Petersburg, confront Bernstorff and the ringleaders of the assassination plot, and persuade them that Britain's certain action against Denmark would render such an assassination unnecessary, and almost certain discovery and death for them all.

'However, there is presently a *ukase* – an edict of the tsar – which forbids foreign nationals from entering or leaving the capital without proper cause. So it was that the baroness – who is nominally a Danish subject – pleaded with me – as consul-general for Andorra – to issue her with a document which would allow her to travel to Petersburg, ostensibly on business relating to Andorra. And this I did.'

'But her mission to prevent the assassination – that failed,' said Oakshott.

'Yes.'

Oakshott took his glass and walked over to the stern windows. The sea, now that the storm had passed, had taken on an almost glassy calm. Of *Pickle* there was no longer any sign.

'And where is the baroness now?' he asked.

'I have no news of her,' replied Constantinopolous. 'But

along with the order that I was restored as accredited Consul-General for His Britannic Majesty in Narva, together with instructions that all British ships were free to enter and leave ports of the Russian empire, and that sequestered British property was restored, there came another item of news.'

'And what was that?' asked Oakshott.

'Bernstorff's part in the assassination plot had been immediately discovered,' said Constantinopolous. 'And he and his associates were summarily executed by firing squad in the mews courtyard of the Summer Palace.

'Why – my dear Oakshott, you have broken your glass, and your hand is bleeding badly.'

Night . . .

Oakshott blessed the darkness, for it enclosed him in a carapace of thought – and he had plenty to think about, God knows.

He stood on his own quarter-deck again, feeling the kick of the sea through his limbs, from toe joints, leg joints, waist, neck – every movable part responding in fine degrees of balance, and all quite unconsciously applied; learned from long experience of that particular ship, and no two ships kick alike.

He took out the letter – *her* letter. There was light enough by the stern lantern to read it; but he had devoured it so often that he could now recite it by rote . . .

Oakshott . . .

Since we shall never meet again, it behoves me to tell you that I have loved you since the moment I first set eyes upon you, since I first heard you speak.

In the Admiralty, I waited for you, for I knew you had been summoned; followed you to that absurd Mogg's so as to look upon you, merely. And when you left, I again followed you, fearful as any schoolgirl to betray myself. My dear, it was only my marvellous agility that helped me to scale that wall, or my secret would have been out there and then.

And by the time you read this, we shall be parted for ever. I have to journey to an appointment with Fate that I could not evade, even if I wanted. But whether I win or lose in this coming venture, this must be the end of what there ever was between us. We are fire and air – mutually destructive.

K.-

Constantinopolous's news was the final brush stroke that had completed the portrait of the woman known as Katerina Jacobson. It was an image that he had part-composed in his mind upon first reading the letter and testing its declarations against hard fact, after the fashion of his logical, mathematical mind.

'*. . . from the moment I first set eyes on you . . . first heard you speak.*'

That could only refer to his meeting with Axel Bernstorff in the dimly-lit after cabin of the *Hedeby*. But she had not been present on that occasion. Or had she? Had she been hiding somewhere in the cabin?

Then – where? And why?

So she had waited at the Admiralty. Followed him to Mogg's. Trailed after him through the snow to Covent Garden – and then escaped him by the remarkable scaling of a high wall.

And after that . . .

His meeting with Bernstorff. And in a sparsely lit room. Seated at some distance, face deeply shadowed.

All in all, he had confronted the creature known as Count Axel Bernstorff on only two occasions, and both times in conditions of near darkness.

It was scarcely likely that a person of her penetrating intelligence would have overlooked the fact that, by a *lapsus calami* – a slip of the pen – she had lifted the edge of the curtain that concealed from the world the vital truth of her living and being. Was it not more likely that she had wanted him to know her secret, and had communicated it to him in such a manner that only he would understand?

Her secret – *that she and Count Axel Bernstorff were one and the same person!*

Javelin was sailing close-hauled now, bending steeply over in the fresh night winds, and the bow wave was reaching its highest point at fully one-third of her length – proof that she was moving at something near her fastest.

Oakshott looked down into the rushing white water sparked with phosphorescent illumination by countless millions of microscopic sea creatures, and was greatly conscious of the multiplicities of life – and death.

He knew – though he would never be sure – that it was she whom he had known as Katerina Jacobson, who had addressed herself to him as Count Axel Bernstorff aboard the *Hedeby*; she who had treated with Pitt, Bonaparte, the Tsar Paul and the rest; she for whom the pursuit of power and the manipulation of kings and princes had meant more than life and love, for which in the end she had been taken out with her fellow conspirators, put up against a wall in a palace mews and shot in St Petersburg.

Oakshott sighed, exchanged a 'good night' with the officer of the watch, and went below to turn in.

ENVOI

A Note to Scholars, Researchers, et cetera